THE SHUFFLE

"*The Vegas Knockout* is a funny book, full of engaging characters that cover the spectrum of human likeability. What makes it more than a piece of fluff is how Schreck uses Duffy's love of boxing to stand in for any devotion truly held. Duffy's success is in his journey, just as the greatest fun in *The Vegas Knockout* is in the reading."

— DANA KING, AUTHOR OF THE PENNS RIVER
CRIME NOVELS

"*Out Cold* floored me with a quick one-two of the serious and seriously funny. Schreck's unique blending of the absurd and the sublime, along with his rather oddball cast of characters, makes *Out Cold* a great read."

— REED FARREL COLEMAN, TWO-TIME
SHAMUS AWARD WINNING AUTHOR OF *EMPTY*
EVER AFTER

"*Out Cold* is a fast, funny, rip-roaring read, and Schreck's wit and humor shine through on every page. But what I love most about Schreck's creation, Duffy Dombrowski, is the decency and dignity with which he treats the unforgettable cast of loonies, addicts, and criminals who parade through his office. I haven't cared this much about a protagonist in a good long while. Duffy is a real hero and a true original."

— BLAKE CROUCH, AUTHOR OF *ABANDON*

"Fresh, intense and funny, Schreck's second mystery to feature unrepentant Elvis fan and dog lover Duffy Dombrowski packs a knockout punch."

— PUBLISHERS WEEKLY, FOR TKO

"Refreshingly iconoclastic."

— KIRKUS REVIEWS, FOR TKO

"*TKO* is fast-paced, authentic, and funny as hell. Social worker and journeyman boxer Duffy Dombrowski is a workingman's hero, and I want him in my corner!"

— SEAN CHERCOVER, AUTHOR OF TRINITY GAME

"Not since Carl Hiassen's *Tourist Season* debut has there been a novel with such superb comic timing and laugh-out-loud lines."

— KEN BRUEN, SHAMUS AWARD-WINNING AUTHOR OF THE GUARDS, FOR ON THE ROPES

"An Everyman with a big heart and a wicked jab, Duffy Dombrowski may well be the new Spenser. I can't wait for Round Two."

— MARCUS SAKEY, AUTHOR OF THE BLADE ITSELF, FOR ON THE ROPES

"*On the Ropes* is sly, funny, irreverent, and one hell of a good time. Read it or be sorry you didn't. It's just that simple."

— LAURIEN BERENSON, AUTHOR OF *HOUNDED TO DEATH*

"It'll put you down for the count with laughter. Tom Schreck is a contender for funniest author working in the crime genre today."

— WILLIAM KENT KRUEGER, AUTHOR OF *THUNDER BAY*, FOR *ON THE ROPES*

THE SHUFFLE

THE DUFFY DOMBROWSKI MYSTERIES

TOM SCHRECK

GLOVES OFF PUBLISHING

THE SHUFFLE

Library of Congress Control Number: 2025926717
Paperback ISBN: 978-1-971208-12-1
Digital Book ISBN: 978-1-971208-13-8

PRINTED IN THE USA

PART I

1

———————

It was five after two on one of those winter days which made you think of retiring to Sarasota even if you hated golf and Florida. The weather geeks were talking about the wind chill, how fast frostbite can come on and the dangers of black ice.

I wiped down the bar and checked to make sure the Bud Light, Blue Moon, and Coors Light were all stocked. The box of red wine which gets poured as often as the Mets win the series probably needed to be replaced, but that wasn't about to get an A-1 on my time management system. That is, if I had a time management system.

Rocco, one of the regulars, was in drinking coffee and doing his annoying habit of reading the New York Post out loud. He was in his late sixties, with short brown hair, on top of a large, sturdy head, a ruddy complexion, and a body made up of hard fat. *Sports Center* played in the background, and they reported on the NFL playoffs with as much energy as the CNN talking heads reported on big deal politicians on trial. It was all tedious.

"Probable serial killer in Staten Island. Dog Saves Drowning Baby in Far Rockaway. Garbage Strike Starting to Stink in Queens."

No response was required.

Every day around 2 p.m. a group of recovering or recovery-wannabees from the clinic where I used to work come to drink free coffee and chat. It wasn't much different than the group therapy I used to run, except I didn't have to do notes or treatment plans or any of that bullshit. There were no rules about attendance or how many times a week you had to come in. People came in and talked and hung out. Less stigmatizing than a clinic and probably just as effective.

Kyrone was in first at 2:10. Punctuality was not a strong suit of most addicted people and here it didn't matter. At the clinic, the director insisted on the clients being on time and equated it with motivation for sobriety and adopting a new lifestyle. I think that was bullshit, too.

"Wassup, D? All good?" Ky and I bumped fists. I gave him his coffee in the mug I kept behind the bar that said "No One Cares, Work Harder."

He proceeded to add about ten packets of sugar to it.

Carl came in after Ky and said hello. He preferred tea. He had on an Izod sweater, turtleneck, wide wail cords, and cordovan loafers with tassels. After him Juan, walked in at the same time with Kaycera, and I got out their mugs, the half and half and the sugar. The group exchanged hellos.

Al, my tri-color basset hound and Agnes, my liver and tan bloodhound, got off their beds and sat behind the group. I produced the mini Milk Bones for their treats. Agnes had belonged to TJ, a woman I had a complicated history with.

Ky threw one to Al. It hit him on the head and he scurried around looking for it. Agnes ate it before he could find it. Al objected and barked. Kay got off her stool and gave one directly to Al.

Next in was Ali. She was around twenty, a light-skinned African American who was painfully thin. She had angular features and an aquiline nose. But her lips were chapped, and her skin was what my black friends called ashy.

Ky, Kay, and Carl got quiet, which was not their usual state. After a long time, Ky spoke.

"Ali, you usin', huh?" It wasn't really a question. It was more of a statement looking for validation.

Ali had that look addicts get when they've been using pain killers. She was here, but not totally here.

She nodded. A single tear ran down from her left eye.

"You've been hurtin' for a while, girl," Kay said and put a gentle hand on her back. Agnes walked closer to Ali, put a paw on her knee, and whined. Ali put her hand over her eyes and started to cry harder.

'I-I-I, it just too much. I wake up wanton' to not use and by three o'clock, it is all I think of." She said and snuggled.

Al walked closer to her, stopped and looked at me as he tilted his head. I shrugged.

"D, you got any rehab connections? You know ways to cut through red tape?" Ky kicked off today's discussion.

"Yeah, my connections might be a little rusty, but yeah, the rehab guys are always around looking for people," I said.

"Ali, will you go again?" Carl asked. His voice was soft.

"Dunno know if you call it a relapse. She ain't never really stopped," Juan said.

"Girl, you're in some trouble." Kay said.

"Ali, are you willing?" I asked.

"I think so," she said through a whimper.

"I think she need to get out of Crawford," Ky said.

"Why not any of the local places?" There were three rehabs

in and around Crawford. St. John's, Evergreen Park and Trinity Health.

"She's been to all in the last year and they didn't work and they aren't making it easy to take her back," Kay said.

I brought the coffeepot over and freshened their cups.

"Might be good for her to get out of town, but she got Medicaid," Ky said.

"Some places will cover travel and everything. I'll look into it," I said. I knew a rep from one of the Florida places. He was a bit of a salesman, but if he could get her in treatment and a way from where she got into trouble, I really didn't care what he was like. "I'll call him right after we're through. For now, let's keep talking."

The rest of the discussion centered around encouraging Ali and trying to build her self-esteem. She wasn't a client at the clinic I worked in. She came after I quit a while ago but got thrown by my former boss Claudia because Ali came in late a lot. Claudia was a stickler for rules, actually lived for them, and enforced them without mercy. She could rationalize discharging Ali because being late is addict "behavior." Claudia and I were not friends.

Ali came from Crawford's ghetto, Jefferson Hill, never really knew her mom and lived back and forth with aunts and uncles.

The group got to talking about Fentanyl, pain, and cravings. Those were Ali's and most of their drugs of choice. Having a close friend relapse was disturbing, but it could be therapeutic because it kept the danger of relapse upfront and real.

Each of them had about four cups of coffee. With the exception of Ali, each of them seemed in a pretty good space and all of them thanked me as they filed out.

"You let me know what you hear from rehabs, okay?" Ky said.

"I'm on it," I said.

"*Drag Queen Kindergarten Tea Party Draws Protest…Central Park Couple Arrested for Doing it at Home Plate on Softball Field…Public Urination Up in the Bronx,*" Rocco continued. "Boy, the world is full of all types, ain't it? Liars, hypocrites and con artists. I guess we all got a little of that in us."

Rocco was waxing a bit poetic.

I hit my playlist after the group left and turned down the TV. Elvis was singing, which wasn't a surprise because it was an all-Elvis playlist.

Cause if there's one thing she don't need, it's another little baby's mouth to feed…

2

———

Donny Bopp used to stop by the clinic when I worked there. He represented in-patient facilities and his job, in plain language, was to "put heads on beds." In the rehab world, a place was successful when it was full and it was the job of guys like Donnie to make sure they were.

Hey, people needed help and Donny got them there. Sometimes, maybe, people went to rehab when they could've done okay staying home and going to outpatient treatment. Sometimes, people who had limited insurance benefits should have conserved those benefits and not use them all up in one rehab stay. But, all-in-all, Donnie did far more good than bad. His shiny Lexus, perpetual tan and Armani suits may have rubbed people the wrong way, but I always got along with him.

Donny even stopped in the bar occasionally. He knew about my informal group. In fact, if it had to do with addictions, he knew about it. It was his business, and he was in his personal recovery, so it was kind of his mission. It was also lucrative.

He was one of those guys who almost had you believing you were one of his best friends. I'm not sure it was an insincere act or just how he was, but he leveraged relationships in his business to get what he wanted. He wanted referrals, and I'm sure in his psyche it was because he wanted to help people and "carry the message to the addict who still suffers," as the Twelve Steps say.

Was he manipulative?

No doubt.

Were we all?

Same answer.

"Duff, my man!" He said when he came in. He did that boxing stance non-boxing people do which is so incorrect it makes fighters shake their heads. He gave me an extra firm handshake and made it clear he'd let go last.

"Hey, Donny. How's things?" I said. I didn't try to match his intensity.

"Still fighting?" he asked, referencing my pro boxing career.

"Well, I'm not retired, but the phone doesn't ring with offers too often." I've been a pro fighter for fifteen years, and I beat the local guys, sometimes good regional guys, but I almost always lost to up-and-comers. It was what the promoters wanted.

"I remember when I played my last game of ball in college. It was hard to walk away from. I liked hitting people. Of course, back then, I had a lot of anger in me," Bopp said. His dialogue always drifted into something recovery related.

Jerry Number Two, another one of The Foursome who were regulars, didn't turn his gaze from *Sports Center*. Jerry was an aged hippie, with a wiry red afro, a roll of fat which showed through his tie-die and wire-rim glasses. He was the only other customer.

"I'm blessed and grateful," Bopp said.

It annoyed me. Not that it was a bad sentiment. Responses

like that seemed to be centered around the message they were doing better than you. Sure, I supposed I felt somewhat blessed and had gratitude for some things, but not strong enough to announce it in my greetings.

"I called because I know someone who needs help," I said.

He took a seat. I gave him a coffee without asking. He turned on the overly concerned and genuine look I kind of thought was neither.

"Talk to me," he came back with.

"Young girl named Ali Estime. She's been coming here with the others to chat…No sober time to speak of. She's burned every local bridge to treatment. She only has Medicaid, and I'm almost positive she hasn't followed any of the recommendations of any of the providers."

Sometimes treatment programs turn clients down for a lack of motivation, which is bizarre to me. I had always thought lack of motivation to quit using drugs was the primary symptom of being addicted.

"I got this, D. Florida sober house. Place called 'Serenity Acres.' It is in Sarasota, beautiful place. She fits the criteria for all of it."

Al came out of the back room. He walked slowly toward Donnie, sniffing. He stopped two feet away and raised his nose, continuing to sniff. I think he was downloading data. He didn't come closer. He suspected Donnie wasn't going to give him a treat. He sat and looked at Bopp.

"What's up with the hound?" Bopp said. "He's not going to attack me, is he?"

"Nah, he's got a funny personality. Sometimes, it takes him awhile to warm up to someone," I said. "Back to Ali, what about the Medicaid issue?" Money was always an issue in the recovery biz.

"No issue at all. Florida is much easier to deal with than New York. Less red tape, fewer barriers to getting help."

Donnie exuded confidence. He gave you the sense everything was going to work. That everything was going to be alright.

I knew things almost never work out.

I knew things were never going to be alright.

"How soon can you get her here?" He said.

"Here? It can happen that fast?"

"I need her card. She needs a packed bag. I'll fly with her myself."

"Who pays for the flight?"

"Serenity covers everything. Get her here. I'll make a couple of phone calls and will save this girl's life." He tapped his knuckles on the bar like everything was all set.

"I'll get right on it. I'll call you when I know more."

Donnie winked and headed out. Al followed him with his eyes, and after Bopp went through the door, Al looked back at me.

He barked once and headed back to his bed.

3

───────

I called Ky and let him know about Donnie. He said he'd get Ali to the bar by seven. I called Donnie and let him know.

"We can get a flight on Allegiant at 9:30," he said. It sounded to me like something he did this all the time.

"That quick? That's it?" I asked.

"Duff, man, you know how this works. Every day gives them another chance to get high. With the shit out there now, that means another chance to get dead."

He was right. I've seen the drug use landscape change drastically in the last fifteen years. It used to be that crack would devastate lives and turn people into ravenous animals willing to do anything for the high.

Today was different.

Now, with opioids being the drugs of choice, you added in a hard-physical withdrawal, a damaged pain tolerance threshold, and the same burning desire to escape, along with the real chance the drug would kill you with one dose.

So much for advancement and progress.

The politicians threw money at it but mostly ineffectively.

Ali was in treatment all the time. Inpatient, outpatient, therapeutic communities, religion-based programs, and don't think she ever strung together three days in a row clean in five years. She had come to our bar sessions, but most of the time, I think she was high. Sweet young woman, but she was a hot mess.

Now she would go to a sober house with counseling every day.

Optimism didn't wash over me.

At a quarter seven, Donnie showed up. Jerry Number One was in now. He had made his career in air conditioning and refrigeration and was now retired. He was heavyset, bald on top, and his upper body was too big for his legs, so he kind of walked hunched over. Rocco was also in and was reading the New York Post. Jerry just drank his Coors' Light and watched *Sports Center*.

Kim, the physical therapist from the neighborhood wearing her Alabama sweatshirt, Abby, the bartender from Burt's downtown, and Patti, who worked for Crawford High School in the cafeteria, were chatting about something and would soon order something from the grill. It was nice a few women filled out the bar once in a while.

"You think she'll show?" Donnie said. He sounded more nervous than I expected. Donnie didn't have a bag, and he wore the suit he had on this afternoon without the tie. He looked at his watch.

"I don't know. Ky is a tough guy to say no to, and he cares. If he said he could get her, he can."

"She's still an addict." Donnie said without explanation. He didn't need one. His implication was addicts weren't responsible or reliable, especially when it involved committing to getting help.

I gave Donnie a cup of coffee and he nodded his thanks.

"You miss working the clinic?" he asked, making conversation.

"I miss the chance to help some people. I don't miss the bullshit paperwork and regulations. I don't miss the patients who didn't have any motivation at all and were gaming welfare."

"You just described ninety-five percent of the job." Donnie said.

"Yeah, it is why I bar tend."

"You have any problem with it?" Donnie said.

"You mean being in the bar business?" I said.

"Yeah."

Right then Ky came in with Ali. Donnie stood up straight and put a big smile on his face. He had a way of smiling which looked authentic even when you knew he was faking it. Ali still had on her ripped jeans and dirty white Crocs. Ky had a small gym bag.

"Wassup, Duff?" He turned toward Bopp. "This is Ali," I nodded. Going off to rehab wasn't a cause for celebration. "I threw some of her stuff in a bag."

Agnes appeared. She walked a semi-circle around the group and got behind Ali. Agnes moved her body into the back of Ali's back legs and stood there.

"Ali, I'm Don Bopp from Serenity Acres. I am so glad you made the decision to save your life." It was corny as hell, but Donnie pulled it off.

She barely nodded.

"Okay, thanks Duff. Thanks Ky. We need to get to the airport." Donnie held out his hand toward the door with the silent command to move out. Ali complied in silence. She hadn't said a word. She hadn't asked a question.

We watched the two of them leave. Agnes lifted her head and witnessed Ali moving out. She whined, turned and looked at me.

I shrugged.

"That's it?" Ky said.

I shrugged.

"Rehab is some wack fuckin' business." Ky shook his head.

I shrugged.

PART II

4

———

It was one-thirty and Kyrone came into the bar. The informal group didn't officially start for another half an hour, and unofficial start was forty to forty-five minutes away.

Something was up.

"She went and left. Two and half weeks and she fuckin' booked," Kyrone said. He was pissed and filled with disgust.

"Whoa, chill," I put my hands in front of me, palms out, in that calming motion which almost never was. "What the hell are you talking about."

"I called to check on her and they said she was AMA," AMA was rehab speak for Against Medical Advice.

"They told you that? They broke confidentiality?" I said. Rehabs can't give out information. Like everything else these days, there need to be signed releases. Kyrone wasn't family, or at least not official family, so I doubted he was listed as a contact.

"They gave it up easy. I just asked twice and told her I was her cousin. The dude on the phone wasn't too professional. He sounded like a punk brother, not no counselor." Ky hadn't calmed at all.

"They tell you anything else?" I asked.

"She split in the middle of the night. Said she wasn't very motivated and wasn't compliant and shit."

"No one is in the first two weeks," I said.

Ky hadn't touched his coffee. He was seething and shaking his head.

"You hear from her?" I asked.

"No. She left the message on voicemail. Said there was some fucked up shit goin' on in this place that was supposed to help you. Said all the other women gettin' high. That they were probably whorin' right in the house."

"What? That's crazy,"

"That's what she said. She didn't sound high either, not that you can tell on the phone."

"What else did she say?"

"Nuthin' really. I tried to call her but now her phone goes straight to voice mail. Don't they usually take the phones away in rehab?"

I gave it some thought.

"Yeah, a lot of times you've got to earn the privilege to make a call," I said. As the words came out of my mouth, I realized how stupid it was.

"That's some fucked up shit, ain't it?" Kyrone looked at me like I made the rules.

"Yeah, I guess. The idea is you don't want patients distracting themselves from their treatment but contacting people on the outside or spending all their time on the phone.

"Distractin' themselves? Who you know, addict or some genius, can stay focused on treatment twenty-four/seven."

I nodded. I didn't have a good answer from that.

"Man, that's some fucked up shit." Kyrone said.

"Will she try to call you?" I asked.

"Dunno, not until after she gets high, that's for sure. Who knows what will happen in the meantime. She got no contacts down there. Who knows what kind of scum bags she'll hook up with to get her shit."

He was right. At least when she was in Crawford, she'd know the lay of the land. It still was dangerous, but she knew the players, and she had some support. In Florida, she was alone and probably on the street.

"I'll call Bopp." I said.

"Man, don't take offense, but that man seemed greasy as fuck." Ky sat back on the barstool and slouched like only he could.

I didn't disagree with him.

5

———

"Ah fuck!" Donnie Bopp said when I called and told him. "How many days was she in?" He was more talking to himself than to me.

"I don't know, it was something like two and a half weeks," I said.

I heard him checking something. I could hear him, but his head and mouth were away from the phone. I figured he was searching through his smart phone.

"Son of a bitch! Seventeen days. Son of a bitch." Again, he wasn't really talking to me. He was just pissed.

"Donnie, is there something magical about seventeen days that pisses you off?"

"Fuck yeah, there is." This wasn't the charmer who spit out all the twelve-step talk. "She leaves before day twenty, I lose my commission."

I didn't know what to say about that. The fact someone got a bonus for getting into drug treatment seemed skeevier than the rest of the business.

"Commission?" I said to keep the conversation going.

"Never mind," Donnie said. "She'll come back. She know anyone down there?"

"Kyrone says she doesn't."

I heard Donnie exhale. I could tell he was frustrated.

"They'll find her. There's one main area the addicts go to. It won't take her long to find it, and then we can pick her up."

"What do you mean, they'll find her? Who is going to go after her?" Rehabs weren't in the business of search in rescue. After all, you had the right to refuse treatment. If it was a condition of probation, you might get it revoked, but it wasn't part of a treatment program to go after patients.

"Duff, this is a matter of life and death. Addiction spares no one. It's either institutions, the mental hospitals or the morgue," Donnie said.

He had regained his composure and was back to regurgitating twelve-step clichés. There was no shortage of them.

"Anything I can do to help?" I asked. It was kind of to be saying something.

"Listen. See if your group hears anything. Even if we can save only one..." Donnie did the pseudo-sensitive helper guy. Honestly, I wasn't sure if he was talking about saving one person or one commission.

"Will do, Donnie. Will do," I said.

"I'll be in touch, Duff"

We signed off.

———

After I locked up, I took Al and Agnes for a walk around the block. It was a Tuesday night, and the air had a bite to it. Al had a spring to his step and pushed out ahead of Agnes and me. Agnes was in Hoover mode and was sniffing the sides of the buildings where the structures met the sidewalk. A city bus cruised by, making the loud exhale and letting out some exhaust. Both dogs stopped and glared at it suspiciously, wondering if any action needed to be taken.

I think I knew how they felt.

Something stunk about this thing with Ali. Troubled young woman, probably from the day she was born, didn't know what it was like to not be high and not much support behind her. Thank God for Kyrone.

I felt so weak when Kyrone or, for that matter, anyone came to me looking for help with addiction. I worked in the field for years, and I couldn't see where treatment helped much. When it got people off the street for a while and kept them physically away from it, maybe that reprieve got them going towards being sober.

At the same time, if you checked them in to the Crawford Hilton and took out the minibar and supervised them for thirty days, it might do the same thing. I don't think the formal group therapy at the clinic did any more than the folks sitting around the bar. I mean, I think it is healthy for people to talk. If that makes them feel better, and they get advice or, if they get a someone to listen and relate and understand—maybe that had something to it. Maybe learning the shit you've been telling yourself for years was wrong, and you didn't have to believe it helped.

Maybe finding something bigger than yourself to get passionate about did something.

I don't know if I had any of those things in my life.

Al let out a baritone bark.

I think he was telling me to get moving.

6

I woke up in the morning feeling a bit groggy. Sleep didn't come easy last night and the Jim Beam and Benadryl had me coasting over sleep instead actually falling into it. I made the coffee, poured it in to my TCB mug and plopped myself on to the leather couch I had inherited from AJ when he gave me the place.

Al took three tries to jump up next to me. On the last one, I hooked my forearm around his butt and hefted him up. He grunted, righted himself and then purposely marched the length of the sofa and walked on to my lap, as if my thigh was just a speed bump. He stretched out precariously on my legs, which were up on the coffee table.

He made a wonderful heated blanket, albeit a significantly weighted blanket.

I put on the TV and went to ESPN. Steven A. Smith was angry about the football playoffs and another black guy, who probably had been a wide receiver, with a great fade and beard, a tweed vest, under a matching tweed jacket and Buddy Holly glasses, disagreed. Everything about it was contrived, and I didn't much care about the football playoffs.

Local news did a live remote from an upcoming holiday craft fair, and that had an interview with a woman who made wreaths out of pine cones. The weather came on and the big blond with the sparkly red evening gown let us know it was going to be overcast and seasonally cool.

It was all insipid.

All of this was my morning routine and the structure of it made me feel like I was doing something when it was only drinking coffee and spending time with Al and Agnes while I procrastinated the start of the day. Agnes didn't stir and was so calm it looked like somehow all her bones had been removed. She ignored the morning routine until she perceived breakfast was going to be late.

The last stop on the idiot box, after ESPN and the local news, was a quick pass through the cable news networks. I had no use for politics, but kind of like checking on the NBA scores I cared less than nothing about, I checked on the various points the right and left were making. That meant MSNBC, CNN and Fox in that order.

I couldn't stomach the righteous snarkiness of Mika and Joe. I didn't know the name of the small hot blond with the tight dress on CNN, but I did know she never smiled, and for whatever reason, that made her smolder even more to me. I spent the least amount of time on Fox, though I did notice their news wasn't as abhorrent as some said it was. They didn't cover the things MSNBC did, but that didn't mean it was wrong. I didn't know enough about it to know who was right and but it did seem like even reporting wasn't the goal.

Joe and Mika were absent and instead there was an aerial

view of a house, probably shot from a helicopter. The scroll said "Mass Shooting at Drug Rehab."

A local Florida reporter was talking to an NBC correspondent. Neither of them knew much yet, but that didn't keep them from talking.

I switched over to CNN and the angry blond was in front of the big screen talking to her man on the scene.

"Ryan, what can you tell us from the scene there in Sarasota?" she said.

"We don't know much at this point. A gunman with an automatic weapon entered the rehab somewhere around two in the morning. It is unclear how access was attained. Then, the gunman opened fired and killed six residents and three overnight staff who were working the overnight shift," he said.

"What type of facility is this? We first got word it was a drug rehab." The blond said.

"Not exactly a rehab. It is what in Florida is called a 'sober house.' Sober houses are residential facilities where people go after they've completed a traditional thirty-day rehab stay," he said.

"The name of the facility?" she asked.

"It is part of the Serenity Acres corporation," he said.

My blood ran cold. Serenity Acres? That was where Ali was. Ky said she split, but what if she had come back or they went and got her like Bopp was suggesting?

The kid goes to get help, and this happens? I didn't get how the world worked.

7

———

They didn't report the names of the causalities. CNN didn't, MSNBC didn't and Fox didn't. NewsMax didn't. No one did.

Ky thought she had split, but Bopp knew the details.

I got on my computer and searched and there was plenty of reporting about the event but nothing about the identities.

Donnie didn't answer when I called. I left a message and requested he call me back as soon as possible. I felt the need to do something, but I had no idea what.

So I called my cop friend Mike Kelley to see what he could tell me about procedures. Kell got promoted to detective awhile back, so I guess he was more than a "cop friend," but that phrase rolled off the tongue easier than "detective friend."

"Kelley"," was all he said when he answered. It was his standard phone greeting. I usually started our conversations by busting his balls about it, but this morning, I didn't feel like kidding around.

"You hear about the mass shooting in Florida?" I said without a preliminary greeting.

"Hard not to. It is all over the news." Kelley's tone was perpetually stuck on annoyance.

"They haven't released any names." I said.

"Yeah. And?"

"Don't they usually do that?" I said.

"The bar business gotten that slow? Don't you have a boxing gym to run? Instead, you're critically watching the news and questioning what they disclose and what they don't?"

"One of the clients who came into the bar was in that place. I got word yesterday she split AMA."

Kelley went quiet. I knew him long enough and well enough to know this meant he was thinking. It also meant he was thinking about me getting involved with something I had no business getting involved in.

"Duffy, what are you doing?" His annoyance went from five to eight on the annoyance meter.

"Nothing. I'm trying to find out what the hell happened and what's going on." I was trying to keep under control.

"In Florida. Two thousand miles away. In a state you don't live in. People you don't know, and there's a young addict who you don't know very well, who ran away from a drug treatment program. Don't they do that more than they stay in those places?"

Now I was getting annoyed.

"Just answer my question, will ya? Do they usually release names?" I regretted my tone.

"Easy champ," Kelley said. He was a good enough friend to give me some slack, maybe even when I didn't deserve it. "It is up to local authorities to release information. Factors which can affect that include whether all the next of kin have been notified, whether they think it will hamper their investigation, and, in this case, the right to confidentiality of the patients. You should know from your former work confidentiality extends beyond death."

"I guess that makes sense," I said.

"Of course, it makes sense. I've been doing this work for twenty years."

"Okay, I got it. Sorry for the attitude," I said.

"No sweat," Kelley said. He paused, then he asked a question.

"Duffy, your little friend who is in treatment there but split…"

"Yeah?"

"She got any history of violence? Any history of using a gun, anything like that?"

"Not that I know of. Why do you ask…hold it. You're not thinking…"

"I'm not thinking anything. I having nothing to do with this. You said she split from the place. People don't split from a place when they have good feelings about it."

I gave that some thought.

"I guess they don't," I said.

8

Kyrone was waiting for me when I opened the front to the bar. I hadn't even prepped yet, and even with as much stimulation as the morning had brought, I still felt undercaffeinated.

"I heard. That shit is some serious fuckedupness," was the first thing he said to me.

"You haven't heard anything from her?" I asked.

"Of course not. I would have told you."

"Yeah, I know."

I got him a cup of coffee and slid the sugar packets container in front of him. He was shifting his weight from side to side.

"What about that greasy motherfucker who brought her down there? What's his name? Boppert?"

"Bopp. I called him. I'm waiting to hear back from him." I tried to think it over. "Ky, where would she go after she split the place? She doesn't know anyone down there, right?"

"Shit, Duff, Ali ain't never been outta Crawford."

"Then where'd would she go?"

He shook his head and looked at me like I was an idiot.

"Damn, Duffy, you worked in the drug business how long? And you gotta ask where'd she go?"

"How would she know where to score?"

"Shit, addicts be like your girl Agnes. They can sniff shit out. Plus, she in a rehab with other addicts. They all talk."

Agnes walked out from the back after hearing her name. She sniffed and walked back. Al did the same thing.

I poured myself a Diet Coke from the tap, mostly to be doing something.

"Can she handle herself on the street?" I asked. The vision of that frail young woman on the street made me shudder.

"C'mon D, she almost lived on the street here in C-town. Just cause we're smaller than Sarasota doesn't mean we nicer. She gotta deal with dealers, thugs, and pimps."

"She trick?" I asked.

"Not that I know of. Got no pimp. Doesn't mean she didn't, you know, hook up with someone who could supply her. That ain't exactly whorin', but it ain't far from it. Just different words."

"Would she?" I felt a little sick asking.

"You know addicts. Depend on how bad she want to get high. I wouldn't put nothing out of the question with no addict. No, sir. No fuckin' way."

"She got enough smarts to find a way home or at least out of there?"

"Ali survived the streets here. She ain't dead. She resourceful. And she nice. If someone took pity on her, someone with a good heart, she could find a way."

"You got much belief in that ever happening?" I said. I finished the Diet Coke.

"Slim and fuckin' none." I poured him more coffee.

"Family?"

"Strung out mother, lives in Pittsfield. Old dinosaur been shootin' shit her whole life. Thirty-five years old. Saw a picture of her once. No teeth, skin like sandpaper, nappy hair. Look seventy."

I took a breath to think.

"Hold it. thirty-five?"

"Was wondering when you were gonna do the math. That's right. She was fourteen, maybe thirteen, when Ali was born."

"Father?"

Ky laughed a joyless laugh.

"C'mon D, you know Father's Day is the most confusing day in the ghetto."

I shook my head.

"You want to take a road trip?"

"Road trip? Where you be goin'?"

"Pittsfield."

9

It was going to be a slow Wednesday, especially during the day, so I asked Billy to cover for me. He was taking mostly night classes these days, finishing up his MSW because he got a job working with teenagers who had behavioral problems.

I helped Billy out a long time ago when he was a nerdy little kid obsessed with being a karate ninja. He was bullied and made fun for it, but he saved my life by chucking one of those martial arts throwing stars into a guy's neck. I was tied to a tree and was about to be tortured and killed.

I've never made fun of karate since.

Instead, I became a role model to Billy and brought him to the boxing gym. Now he's a respected MMA guy who wants to help others. I'm proud of how I helped him and his mom out. He stopped being made fun of and pretty soon, after hanging in the boxing gym, kids stopped picking on him. I felt good about that and Billy has stayed true to me. He made money bartending, but I think he helps me out because he's grateful.

He's grateful. Did I mention he saved my life?

Life is funny.

Ky and me took the hour and half ride to Pittsfield. Ky doesn't spend a lot of time in silence, so the time flew by. We covered a lot of territory, and the conversation went like this.

"Hey D, all that boxing, has it messed up your thinking?" He asked.

"I don't think so. I wasn't all that sharp before I started. But I also think the damage to the brain takes years to show up." I replied.

"Duff, how come you ain't got no woman?" Ky didn't really hold back when it came to the uncomfortable.

"Well, I had this one woman, TJ. She had issues. We tried to make it work. I thought it was working, and she just left," I said. It was the concise version.

"How come she left?"

"Um, she's in military. Secret shit. Had a husband, thought he killed himself, then he came back. She wasn't sure she wanted a relationship," I said. I hadn't talked about this in a while.

"That fuck you up?" Ky said.

"Yup."

"You said she was in the military. What was she doing around here?"

"She went into the reserves. Then she went back into the active military. She came from a family of military."

"What she do in Crawford?"

"She was a stripper at The Taco. That joint outside of town."

"Whaaaat!" He strung it out so lasted a long time.

"Yup," I said.

"Strippin' fuck her up?" Ky said.

"Nah, I don't think so. She could distance things, and the money was awesome."

"You hear from her?" Ky's voice softened.

"Every now and then. It is sort of unpredictable," I said.

"Man, that's the hardest…"

"Yup," I said.

We moved on to recovery questions.

"Duffy, people who ain't addicts, how they different?" Ky had a genuine curiosity in his voice.

"What do you mean?" I said.

"I only know addicts and people trying not to be. What are normal people like?"

It was a tough question to field.

"Um, I guess there's more in common than there is different. Some non-addicts get high, but it doesn't fuck up their lives. Some deal with things by avoiding shit and working all the time, eating too much, watching internet porn, running, boxing, collecting shit, binging on TV…" I trailed off.

"You mean everyone trying to take their mind off a life?" Ky asked. He had a little desperation in his question.

"Or death. I read a book once called *The Denial of Death*. The writer said all the shit we do while living is to take our minds off the fact eventually our existence will end. We'll die, get buried, and become worm food."

Ky got quiet.

"You believe that, D?"

"I guess on some level I do. I think a better way of thinking about it is to kind of say, 'Shit, we're here and I don't know what it all means. I might as well do shit that matters to give this bullshit some meaning. Maybe help someone along the way.'"

"Word." Ky said. It was that one-word validation which has grown from a ghetto term to the mainstream.

"I read another book written by a guy in a concentration camp. He said finding a cause bigger than yourself was the key to making this livable. If that included helping someone, it made it even more powerful." I was referring to Frankl's *Man's Search for Meaning*.

"He came up with that in a concentration camp? Man had some focus!"

"Not only that, Ky, he came up with it after the Nazis did experimental surgery on him with no anesthesia. He said that made him free," I realized I was lecturing. Ky didn't seem to mind.

"How'd that make him free?"

"He said at that moment, he knew they could hurt him physically, but they could never touch or hurt him spiritually," I said.

"Ain't that some shit! D, can you hook me up with that book?" He was looking right at me.

"Yup," I said.

"That woman, TJ, she keep you from seeing other women?"

I wasn't crazy about the topic. It took me awhile to answer.

Ky looked at me. "Am I gettin' too close?' he said.

He was way too close, but I tried to be open with him because if I was, I thought he might be open with me.

"Um, yeah, I think she does," I took a breath. "Not sure I ever admitted to myself until now."

"Maybe you do that on purpose."

I didn't know what he meant.

"Huh?"

"Like you don't have to try, put yourself out there, maybe get hurt because you can say you're hung up on this TJ. Keeps you safe."

"Safe? You saying I'm scared?" It came out more defensive than I wanted it to be.

"Shit, after some of the crazy shit I know you done over the years, helping people and all that time in the ring, I know you ain't a coward. Not when it comes to danger that could fuck up your body. But…"

He trailed off.

"But when it comes to shit that might tear you up on the inside, maybe you get a little, I don't know…"

"Scared." I finished the sentence for him.

10

———

If your image of Western Massachusetts conjures up Norman Rockwell's America complete with barber shops, bakeries with adorable white boys looking longingly at pies in windows and gingham dresses on darling young women—pump the breaks.

Pittsfield is a shit hole. It was like the whole town needed a good power washing with Gain.

Ky had an address Ali had given him, and it took us to the center of town. Pittsfield didn't have office buildings of any merit, and the main street, fittingly called Main Street, looked like it hadn't been updated since LBJ decided not to run for reelection. Don't mistake what I am saying. It wasn't charming in that old school way. It was dilapidated in that way urban areas go through a slow rot.

It was warmer than it should have been for December, and the sky was grey. It was the type of weather which was impossible to dress for. The hoodie was too warm, and a t-shirt left me with a bit of chill. The address took us up a hilly street, the kind where the houses are built on a slant. Litter lined the streets and the tiny spaces in front of the houses had turned over garbage cans without lids, discarded cardboard boxes and empty quart bottles of beer. It is important to note they were quart bottles. One house had a toilet in front of it near the curb. It was missing the seat, and it made me wonder why.

Ali's mother's address, or at least the address we had for her, was 72 Barrow Street. It was three quarters up the hill, and I could feel my body labor a bit heading up it.

"This be some shit neighborhood. This what pass for a New England ghetto?" Ky said.

"Pretty much," I said.

At 72, there was a woman sitting on a stoop. She was barefoot, wearing blue sweatpants with a series of holes on the thighs which looked like cigarette burns. Weating a man's white wife beater, it was clear she hadn't bothered with a bra. She had chapped lips and drew hard on the Newport, holding the nearly empty pack in her left hand and smoked with her right. She had a do rag on and held her head in her hand.

She looked beyond us with a vacant stare.

"Elaina Estime?" I said.

She sort of laughed or snickered.

Slowly, her eyes seemed to try focusing on Ky and me.

"Nobody call me that except police and DSS," she said police with an emphasis on the O. "People call me E-hi."

I could only imagine why.

"E, we're trying to find Ali," I said. I just put it out there, not knowing how long this conversation was going to last.

"Oh lordy, lordy, that girl…"

"Has she been in touch?" I asked.

"Oh yeah, she be in touch. She speak to me every night"."

She made a sweeping hand gesture while she looked at the sky, forgot about the cigarette and brought that to her lips for a drag.

Ky looked at me. He shrugged his shoulders.

"She come down from the heavens every damn night. She on fire and let's me know Satan is waiting for me. Yes, he is. Lucifer is awaitin.' He just a hopin' to come get me."

Oh boy. I've been around enough mental health folks to know this was going to be largely a waste of time.

"E, she ever call you on the phone?"

"What phone." She turned angry all of a sudden. "I ain't got no motherfuckin' phone. That bitch Sugar took my phone."

Ky looked at me again.

"Before that, did you hear from her?"

She lit a new Newport.

"She call once in a while. She high as can be."

I was regretting the drive over here.

"How about her father? She stay in touch with him?"

She glared at me, took a long drag, pinched something out of her tongue, and spit on the stair next to her.

"You think I can be like Michelle Obama?" She laughed. She laughed really hard.

I didn't say anything. I just looked at her.

"That girl got it goin' on! Love dem arms. I gonna be like her. Yes, I surely fuckin am."

Didn't know what to say to that.

"You got any money? I'm investing in a hedge," she said. Not a hedge fund, a hedge.

I gave her a ten.

"Yes sir, seen one of dem UFOs last night. I think Ali was on one. She flying back to me. That girl flying with the aliens. I miss the old jams. You listen to Lisa One-Eye?"

"Not so much," I said. Ky looked at me. His eyebrows were up.

This dumpster fire was going downhill fast. She talked to Ali her every night, but she had no phone, and Ali only called once in a while. She wanted to be like Michelle Obama. She saw UFOs, and Ali was probably on them. And Lisa One-eye was her favorite.

Heck of a road trip.

It was time to head home.

11

———

Ky and me were quiet for the first half of the ride back. I wasn't sure what to say. I didn't know if I should talk about Ali being missing, the mass shooting, or our meeting with Elaina.

Ky broke the quiet.

"Is it even possible for a baby born from a girl who was thirteen or fourteen to not be all fucked up?" I wasn't sure if it was a rhetorical question, so I waited a bit.

"Can't be," Ky answered his own question.

"Hard to picture a young teenage girl having the skills to mother," I said. It sounded too social worky, and I didn't like it.

"And being in the ghetto doesn't help," Ky added. "What would a baby need in a situation like that to not be fucked up?"

"I don't know. Maybe strong adults in her life. A good grandmother or grandfather, a friend of the family who cared, maybe even the father or the father's family."

"Shiiiit," Ky said. He strung it out over four syllables. "What about the thirteen-year-old mom? Is there anything at all she could try to be for the sake of the kid?" Ky was growing more frustrated. I sensed he was putting to words his frustrations with his own upbringing and what he had been around his whole life.

"She could have a sense of motherhood, I guess. Like, maybe she had something in her that loved the baby so much she devoted herself to her. Maybe the love would be felt, and that would mean something," I said. Now I sounded way too hopeful.

"Or the thirteen-year-old could start really getting high to deal with the shit. Or the thirteen-year-old would continue acting like a thirteen-year-old, and the baby would be, at best, like a pet dog. How that baby gonna grow up to have a chance?"

"I guess we have that answer when it comes to Elaina and Ali." I didn't like how that statement felt. It was like I summarized two lives as complete wastes. It felt wrong.

"Ali is a good girl. She an addict, no doubt, but she nice, you know. She don't steal, she don't whore, she don't curse. How'd that happen?"

I shrugged. The topic was exhausting me. Driving with a guy who lived it and was trying to figure it all out made it that much harder.

I got a call, and I was grateful for the distraction.

It was Bopp.

"Duffy, it's Bopp. What can I do for ya?" He was back on point. Six dead, a girl missing and he was back selling.

"Any news on Ali? She wasn't back in the house for the shooting, was she?"

"No, she hasn't turned up," Bopp said. It was odd. There was a mass shooting in the place he represented, and he didn't have much to say about it.

"How's everyone doing down there?" I felt like I should ask.

"What do you mean?"

I paused.

"The shooting..." I said.

"Well, it has shaken folks up, obviously." He was ridiculously matter of fact.

"I'm sorry." I felt like I had to say something.

"Thank you."

"Um, do they know who did it?" It felt a little insensitive and slightly off topic, but the silence was making me feel a little creepy.

"They have some people of interest. They've looked at the cameras."

Cryptic. It bothered me.

"Who they looking at?" I asked.

"The shooter wore a hooded sweatshirt and a mask. It is hard to say."

I waited.

"I tell you this though, Duffy. Your little friend left her plenty mad and saying some shit about her getting back at people. And the image on the video fits her size and shape."

I didn't know what he was talking about.

"What?"

"Ali is missing. She left angry and was threatening staff. No one can find her."

"You're saying she's wanted for the shooting."

"Yes." Bopp said.

12

"No, no, no...that shit is, no..." Ky said after I relayed Bopp's message.

"You ever know her to have a gun or use a gun?" I asked.

"C'mon D, you saw her. She an addict. She ain't nuthin' else."

"What if somebody did her wrong? She split that sober house for a reason. It wasn't because she was enjoying herself."

Ky looked at me like I was crazy. He rolled his eyes and shook his head in an exaggerated way.

"What would she do? You know what she'd do. She'd get high more. That's all." He had raised his voice and put a bit more bass in it.

"Alright, alright, I get it. So why do they think that?" It wasn't really a question for Ky.

The rest of the ride was strained. Both of us were frustrated, and I sensed it wasn't all about Ali. It was also about the feeling of powerlessness. We couldn't do anything about something we really wanted to fix. For me, it was a familiar feeling and one which drove me. It drove me even when I didn't want it to.

Around the New York State line, it started to snow. It was the type which came from a grey sky, that you knew wouldn't accumulate. It didn't affect the driving of my vision, but it wasn't a pretty snow. It was the type which came from a lot of grey and didn't brighten anything up.

I let Ky off on the corner of Central and Lexington. He said he was going to catch an NA meeting. After the kind of day we had, I saw that as a good idea. It felt a little weird because I sensed I could benefit from a meeting where people would listen and be supportive. There was a lot about the Twelve-Step programs I didn't like, but to have a predictable group of people ready to listen to you seemed like a damn good idea.

I had the gym, and I went there. I was in charge of the Crawford YMCA's boxing program after my mentor and father figure, Smitty, went down south to take care of his nephew. Really, I didn't want to run the gym, but I had been going there since I was twelve years old and cared about the place. When it fell into some disarray with some bad characters and an ugly feel, folks looked to me. Reluctantly, I took over, trying to run things the way Smitty would. So far, so good.

As I came down the stairs, I heard the familiar staccato rhythm of the speed bag tap-tap-tapping with the bass sound of the heavy bag in the background. A few fighters were skipping rope, and that added a hi-hat sound to complete the tune.

Lorenzo was standing with his arms folded, leaning against the door to my office. He was one of the bad guys at the gym who originally came around as a disturbing influence. Now he was my number two in command and the guy I relied on to look after the gym when I wasn't there. He was also a promising, if not reluctant, heavyweight contender. Reluctant because he put his work with the kids ahead of his own career.

His mentee, Trevon, was in, and he was shadow boxing. Tre was now 9-0 as a junior amateur, and when we went to his fights, 'Zo was his chief second. I acted as 'Zo's assistant. 'Zo was hesitant at first to take that role, but I explained to him it meant the most sense because Trevon saw him as such a role model.

Piggy, a forty-something old timer in the gym, was banging the heavy bag with body shots that shook the whole gym. Pig was hard fat and worked in the Steamfitters Union. No one tried to mess with Pig who had any sense, because you could punch him right in the face, and he would barely wince. He'd then hit you in the liver with one of those left hooks, and you wouldn't go to the bathroom right for the next month.

Malik, an on-again-off-again pro, was skipping rope. At thirty-three, he was running out of time, and his job as a hall monitor at McDonough High was always going to pay him more than his boxing career. A few other guys were in and working at the sound of the bell and then resting for the minute interval at the end of each round. Such was the ebb and flow of the gym.

My friend Trace had come in for a workout. Malik would spar with him, giving him good work, hitting him but not punishing him. More proficient fighters would spar with lesser boxers and both would benefit. The better fighter would burn calories and work their cardio while perfecting technique. It was better than punching a static heavy bag.

The lesser fighter would be challenged and be made to leave their comfort zone by facing more advanced technique safely. They'd still get hit but in a controlled fashion. This was precisely how boxers improved.

I watched the sparring. It was high-quality stuff. Malik was working on cutting off the ring and trying to corner Trace. Trace was working on slipping out of the technique without catching a hook meant to coral him back in Malik's wheelhouse. I could see Trace improving.

Trace was not your typical fighter. Honestly, he wasn't a typical anything. He graduated from Notre Dame with a PhD in psychology, worked as a consultant for the CIA, and counseled agents who had to view disturbing terrorist videos and bombings and things like that. He also conducted research.

And because that sort of stuff isn't enough and could be seen as a little boring, he also bartended at his family's tavern in Albany, Curran's. His dad ran the place for years and died a little while back. Trace had gotten a little fucked up over an engagement gone bad and his own PTSD from shit that went down.

I could relate.

"Sup Trace?" I said, and we bumped fists. He was done in the ring and was undoing his hand wraps, which was a sign he was winding down.

"Working with Malik is awesome. The freakin' guy can adapt to anything," he said, marveling at the more experienced fighters' skill.

"He's a pro. That's what they do."

"Yeah, lets me know how far there is to go," he said, shaking his head.

"For all of us. For every one of us."

Trace laughed.

"What cool spy shit are you working on now?" I said, changing gears.

"Usual stuff on the caseload. Agents dealing with some shit. In the research area, I'm on a team looking at mass shootings," he said.

"No shit!" I said.

"You hear about this latest one in Florida?"

"Of course, the sober house."

"I helped a young woman get admitted there a couple of weeks ago. She went AMA just before the shooting. I found out she may be a person of interest."

"Yeah, I got an email about it. Ali Estime, right?" Trace said.

"Yup, that's her."

Trace toweled the sweat from his face. It took a while to cool down after sparring.

"The committee is having a lot of back and forth on it because she doesn't fit any of the usual characteristics or profiles of a mass shooter."

"What are the characteristics other than the neighbor saying they were quiet and like everyone else?"

Trace chuckled at that.

"Actually, as you probably would guess, the shooters vary wildly in their motivations. For some, it can be explained simply because they were severely mentally ill and had a break. For some others, it has to with some sort of revenge, usually around being what they felt as disrespect. And there are others who probably do it for some twisted desire for attention. Or it could be a combination of all of that," Trace said.

"I guess she was angry at the place, but she has no history of severe mental health problems, nor does she have any history with guns," I said.

"There's a wide statistical disparity in the shooters. The commonalities aren't hard and fast.

"It didn't feel right, right from the beginning," I said.

"If had to say a hard yes or no, I would say she doesn't fit the profile. It is almost never females and almost never people with no history of firearms involvement."

13

I got back to the bar at 6:45, which means I was fifteen minutes late. As the owner, maybe that shouldn't bother me, but it meant I held up Billy. He had studying to do and his mom to take care of. He was standing behind the bar with his hands spread right in front of Rocco.

"The buffalo is an animal found in Africa. The animals we have in America are actually bison," Rocco said.

"I don't think that's right," TC said.

"If they are bison, why isn't the city in western New York called Bison?" Jerry Number One said.

"Billy, can I get an order of Bison hot wings to go?" Jerry Number Two said.

At least, this was a new topic. Perhaps they had kicked this around before, but I didn't remember it. I could've been drunk or changing the lines in the basement or focused on *Sports Center* and missed it.

"It was on Jeopardy last night, wasn't it Pasquale?" 'Squal was the big former lineman who bounced at The Taco. A couple of years ago he appeared on Jeopardy and actually was a one-day champ. He drank Narragansett, which I stocked especially for him.

"It was. I believe the answer was 'Commonly referred to as buffalo, this large mammal is actually called this in North America.'"

"Wasn't that the question?" TC said. The Foursome never quite nailed down the answer/question thing on Jeopardy.

"Bison." Rocco replied with authority.

"What is Bison?" Jerry Number Two said.

"Buffalo," Jerry Number One said.

I had gotten behind the bar and slapped Billy on the back.

"Sorry I'm late again," I said. "I got caught up in something at the gym."

"And miss this?" Billy held his hand out palm up in the direction of the Foursome. "By the way, your buddy from Vegas, Boggsy, called. Said he was checking in."

That made me smile. Boggsy helped me out in Sin City a few years back. He was a stagehand at The International and met Elvis a few times. It was just one of the many reasons I revered him.

Lester Holt had come on with the national news, and that interrupted the bison/buffalo debate, which I was confident would resume in the near future.

"We open tonight in Sarasota, Florida, where an explosion at a sober house has leveled a building, killing six residents and four staff. This coming two weeks after a mass shooting killed eight in a sober house in the same organization." Lester threw it to Miguel Almaguerre.

"Tonight, Sarasota residents are in shock and another tragedy rocks the region still grieving from the mass shooting just two weeks ago. Those in the recovery community are devastated."

They then got a statement from someone named "Murray" whose title was "In recovery."

"You know, getting clean shouldn't mean risking your life. This is out of hand." I wondered if Murray had his own communications office, and he was the go-to source on all things recovery.

Next was the governor.

"We have all our resources searching for the perpetrator of the mass shooting while we investigate the cause of this explosion. I would like to remind the people responsible Florida is a Stand Your Ground state and as they roam considering creating violence and mayhem, to remember armed Floridians will not tolerate their lawlessness," he said.

The guy was a likely presidential candidate. He waved his finger in a forceful way at the camera and did his best to look intense. He had wavy brown hair and sharp features with thick eyebrows and the appropriate amount of tan for a Florida politician. Yet he had a weak jawline which seemed to meld into the collar of his white shirt. He was tieless because it was early evening and that was the look. Like he was sitting down to dinner with his loving wife, 2.5 children, and his Labrador when he was called to the press conference.

"Governor, are there any new leads on the shooting?"

"We have a person of interest, a disturbed woman who abruptly left the program shortly before the shooting. She is unstable and probably still armed. She should be viewed as dangerous," he said as earnestly as he could.

Was he referring to Ali? A hundred pounds of scared addict

who knew nothing in life other than getting high? Dangerous? Disturbed? Armed?

Something wasn't right.

"What's a Stand Your Ground State?" TC asked.

"Means you can shoot anyone on your property," Rocco said. "Like you should be able to."

"Like when the six-year-old kid next door accidentally kicks his soccer ball on to your property?" Jerry Number Two said with a hint of sarcasm.

"Fuckin soccer…" Rocco said.

"Actually, the Stand Your Ground laws have an important clause in it. You can use deadly force when you reasonably believe you are in danger of a violent crime," Pasquale said.

"Like that bastard little kid with the soccer ball," Jerry Number Two said.

"Fuckin' kickball. Wussy sport," Rocco said.

"Well, how can you tell you're in danger? Let alone reasonably tell?" TC said.

"Therein lies the problem," Pasquale said.

"Look, a big Black guy you don't know shows up on your lawn with a dark hoodie he isn't selling Girls Scout cookies," Rocco said.

"Exactly," Pasquale said.

"What do you mean 'Exactly,'" TC said.

"In Rocco's last comment, which, by the way, is how many Americans think, are three assumptions about danger that shouldn't be factored in at all," Pasquale said matter-of-factly.

"Huh?" TC said. This was going kind of fast for the Foursome.

"Rocco said, "One: Big; Two: Black; Three: Guy; Four: Wearing a hoodie. Actually, that's four assumptions. None of these should legally be a reasonable sign of danger," Pasquale said.

"Well, would be a reasonable sign of danger?" TC said.

"Individual with a weapon. Individual verbalizing threats. Individual destroying property." Pasqual gave everyone a look. "You see the difference?"

"You have to focus on the real threat, not your assumptions," Jerry Number Two said.

14

———————

The news cycle was a curious thing. The next morning, there was a smattering of reports on the explosion. By late the next day, none of the major news outlets, network or cable, had anything more to say about the shootings or the explosions. I went online to the Sarasota News to see if they had any more detail. There wasn't much, but I did find this article.

Sober Houses Have History of Issues

Sarasota—The recent tragedies at two Serenity Acres facilities have brought the treatment concept under scrutiny. Unlike traditional thirty-day facilities, in which patients receive medical care, detoxification, group, individual, family and educational treatment, the process of care at sober houses is a bit murkier. Sober Houses are less time-constrained, are staffed with more para-professionals than certified therapists, and rely on what they call the therapeutic milieu of living with other addicts in a supported environment. Frequent urine testing is said to keep residents honest, and they are encouraged to attend 12-Step meetings both onsite and in the community.

Most payment comes from Medicaid or Medicare, and since the Obama Healthcare Act, access to these benefits has become less stringent. The goal of cutting the red tape was to lift the barriers to people getting help. Critics claim it also opened the door to unscrupulous businessmen who saw it as an easy cash grab.

The current drug problem in the United States has reached epidemic proportions with a 26% increase of fatal overdoses in the last three years. Some blame the proliferation of legal pain killer drugs, which are frequently over-prescribed. The highly addictive drugs leave pain victims addicted quickly, and when their medication runs out, they seek relief, often settling for street heroin.

The Purdue Pharma company, owned by the Sackler family, was found to have knowingly marked the drugs as pain killers for anyone dealing with pain. Originally, drugs like OxyContin and Fentanyl were designed for dying cancer patients. Patients in hospice and palliative care do not have to be cautious about addiction because they are in the last stages of life.

The shift to marketing toward anyone suffering with pain was a deliberate action by Purdue. They have been ordered to pay $10 billion in a settlement for this, but many suggest the sum barely touched the damage that was done. In Florida, where regulations are lax, many pain clinics have sprouted up to fill the need of the addicted. The clinics are lucrative, but many see them as thinly veiled legal drug suppliers that continue to fuel the epidemic.

Politicians eager to create an image they are addressing the problem have fast tracked many corporations including companies like Serenity Acres whose parent company is Humility Inc, which in addition to sober houses runs several inpatient rehabs and several outpatient clinics.

The latest tragedies are, of course, a separate issue, or so it would appear. Still, it is likely the sober house concept will once again be examined.

I thought about Bopp. Perhaps I gave him too much credit, and the idea he was a businessman was overshadowed by the fact he may have been a willing participant in something that may have been unscrupulous or even nefarious.

I called him.

"What's up Duffy?" He was more upbeat than he should have been.

"I'm sorry to hear about the explosion," I said. It felt hollow.

"Awful. Just awful. Two unspeakable tragedies so close together. It is hard enough to get sober."

Always with the recovery talk.

"How are people dealing?" I said.

"They are keeping on. It isn't an excuse to drink or drug." These clichés seemed to come out on automatic pilot.

"Uh, Bopp, that article in the Sarasota News..." He cut me off.

"Bullshit, Duff, utter bullshit. That writer has had it in for us for years. He's an untreated alcoholic himself. I know that firsthand." Bopp was getting fired up. "I wouldn't send one of your people to a bad place, Duff. I hope you don't ever think that."

I didn't say anything.

"Duffy, tell me you don't believe that nonsense. Have I ever given you reason to doubt me?"

I thought about that for a second.

"No, Bopp, you haven't."

"Good! Duff, I gotta run. I got a meeting. Stay in touch."

I signed off.

Maybe he never gave me reason to doubt him, at least, up until to now.

15

———————

The two o'clock group came in at 2:13.

Juan was first, then Carl, then Kaycera and with them was a new guy, Mike. Mike looked like a laborer, a white guy with a ruddy complexion and a build which suggested functional strength, not weights. He wore a Carhartt jacket, dusty Levi's, and work boots broken in and had been obviously used for, well, work.

"This is Mike," Carl said. "Mike this is Duffy, he owns the place. He used to work at the clinic."

I extended my hand. "Nice to meet you, Mike, welcome."

Mike looked around with a look of suspicion.

"Little weird doin' this in a bar ain't it?" He said.

I put a cup of coffee in front of him, the half and half and the sugar.

"It's cool. Just hang out," Kaycera said.

Mike nodded and took a seat.

"Where's Ky?" I asked.

They all shrugged. There was nothing mandatory about these

meetings, but it was unusual if Ky didn't come. He was the one to lead people here.

"Duffy, I notice myself getting really pissed off over little things. My cat knocked over the sugar bowl at my apartment this morning, and I lost it, screaming and cursing," Carl said. He didn't usually lead off.

"When I find myself doing that shit, I try to kick back and ask myself what's really pissing me off. That's me. Not saying you're in denial or shit like that," Juan said.

They looked at me. I did my best to let them find their own answers. Instead of saying anything, I shrugged and looked around.

"What do you think is really pissing you off?" Mike, the new guy, said. He was a bit tentative, like he wasn't sure if he should talk yet.

Carl frowned and shook his head.

"That's just it, Mike. Things are going good. I don't really have anything to be pissed off at." Carl sipped his coffee. Today he had on Khakis and Ralph Lauren pull over. The starched collar of the white shirt stuck perfectly out of the top of the pullover.

"Shit, I don't need no special reason. I can come up with a list on the spot," Kaycera said.

"For real?" Juan said.

"Uh-huh. You want to hear it?" Kaycera made her eyes go wide. She had her hair pulled off her face into a bun. Her brown eyes shone and her mocha-colored skin was smooth except for a half an inch scar on her left cheek.

"I mad I'm an addict. Why can't I get high once in a while like my high school friends? Why can they party on Fridays and

Saturdays and leave it alone? Why don't they have to get high all day, every day, when they usin'?"

"I hear that," Juan said.

"I ain't even close to being done. Why does my grandmother, the woman who raised me like a mother, why does she have to be in a nursing home with dementia? That lady a saint—why'd that happen to her?"

Carl was locked in, looking at her.

"Why does every man I got involved with cheat on me? Why wasn't I born someplace where everyone went to college and didn't wind up in prison instead? Why did I have to have a daughter at sixteen? Why...why...why...shit is fucked up."

"My life has been easier than yours. I'm not from the ghetto. My parents supported me. I went to college..." Carl let it trail off. "Your anger is...is...justified. I don't have the right..." He let it trail off again and looked down at his coffee.

"You sure about that, Carl? Ain't you an addict too? You happy about that shit? Here we are in the middle of the day talking about our shit while other people are out livin'. You're a gay man. Ain't you mad about that? I mean, not about bein' gay, but because of all of the fucked-up people in the world givin' you shit about it? And what about your folks? Sure, you went to college, had nice things, but you told us you could never let them know that you're gay. Ain't that somethin' to be mad about?"

Carl started to cry. It blurted out of him, and he held his hand over his eyes as it intensified. Kaycera got up and stood in front of his stool, put her arms around him until he stood up. Carl shook as he was held.

The others were transfixed. Agnes came over and stood looking at Carl and whined.

No one said anything.

I believed intense moments like this changed a person. In the moment of insight, when the pain rushed up, you begin to realize shit you've been pushing down. It was tough to feel it, but it changed you. Some would find it too intense and run from it, maybe go get high. But they'd be forever changed.

The front door opened.

Ky came in with his usual bop but slowed when he saw what was going on. He'd been around it before and respected it. He stood off from the group solemnly with one hand over the other like a soldier at rest.

Carl's crying slowed, and Kaycera gradually broke off the hug and looked at Carl's face.

"Maybe it wasn't the cat," he said.

The joke broke the tension, and they all laughed.

Ky joined the group.

"Where have you been?" Juan said.

Ky looked around at everyone, then spoke.

"Ali called me."

16

"Said that place was messed up," Ky said. "Didn't make no sense. People getting' high, urine screens every day. She thought the staff were high, maybe even dealin'."

"Whoa, whoa…slow down…" I said. It was tough to process everything he was saying.

"She said strange men coming in like they're boyfriends of the girls living there. They makin' her sign forms for treatment like psychologists, physical therapist, even a dentist and then she don't see none of them." There was no stopping him.

"That's some fucked up shit," Juan said.

"She hurt?" Carl asked. "I mean physically. Is she in any danger?"

"She thought she was in some danger. Said they didn't like her questioning things. One staff said she better get in line and gave her a look. She knew what it meant," Ky said.

"Duffy, could a rehab type place be that bad?" Kaycera asked.

"I mean, I've known of some incompetent places. Places where the staff was getting high, but they were recovering staff who relapsed, not openly using," I said. "I can't say it would be impossible, and places can go downhill, but this sounds like something else."

It sounded lame. It was almost like I was defending the place.

"Is there any chance Ali is, uh, not being completely honest?" Carl said. I got the sense he was uneasy with what he probably thought was judgmental.

The group was quiet. No one touched their coffee. It was a long moment.

Kaycera broke the silence.

"I lied all the time when I was using," she said.

"Word, so did I," Ky said.

"I lied about things that didn't even matter," Carl added.

"Yeah, I did. Shit, we're addicts, of course we did." Juan frowned, then changed the topic. "She say where she was?"

"Uh-uh, she said she didn't trust the phone line. Said they might be listening," Ky said.

"You think she's paranoid?" Kaycera said. "Like from crack?"

"I dunno. It didn't sound that way, but her connection wasn't good," Ky said. "Pretty sure it was a burner phone."

"She say anything about the shooting? Did she know about it?" Juan asked.

"Said she was getting set up. That she wasn't near the place, but that they were coming for her and setting her up," Ky said. "What does your man Bopp say?" Ky looked at me.

"To be honest, he was really low key about it, like it wasn't a big deal. It was strange," I said.

"Mass shooting and a bombing at facilities he represent and he was low key?" Carl asked.

I nodded.

"That seem right to you?" Kaycera said.

"That man seem greasy as shit," Ky said.

"Maybe he ain't the guy to be asking about Ali," Kaycera said.

I think Kaycera was right.

Around 3:30, the group headed back to their lives. Rocco and Jerry Number Two were in by the late afternoon. Rocco had a scotch and soda in front of him, and Jerry had a Cosmo. As usual, Rocco had The Post, of course, while Jerry was reading a Charles Bukowski book.

"Alphabet City Sees Surge in LGBTQ Related Assaults... Bronx Legislator Caught With Hand In the Till...Florida Governor Calls to Gun Owners..."

I was stocking Pasquale's Narragansett when that last one caught my attention.

"Hey Rock, what was that last one about?" I said.

"Huh?" Rock was in his trance and wasn't accustomed to someone bringing him out of it.

"The Florida Governor?"

"Oh, something about, he said at a press conference that gun owners should be on the lookout for the little girl who shot up the one sober house and probably blew up the other one,' Rocco paraphrased the article.

"He said that? The little girl?" I said.

"Yup." Rocco said.

"The governor is calling on Florida gun owners to be on the ready for Ali?"

"Ali? The little girl who came in here that you helped out?" Rock actually put down The Post, which was a sure sign things had gotten serious. "He saying she's responsible?"

"Sure sounds like it," I said.

17

———

The Foursome, Kelley, and Pasquale were all in that night. They were kicking around a new topic.

"They aren't cute. In fact, they are responsible for more fatalities than sharks," Rocco said. He had some force behind his voice.

"C'mon, those fat bastards couldn't catch anyone," TC said. I could never tell if he really disagreed or if he liked to piss Rocco off by invalidating his claims.

Al and Agnes slowly walked out from the back. That sat directly behind The Foursome. It was like they had season's tickets on the 50-yard line.

"Actually, Rocco's right. Hippos are ruthless," Pasquale said. He wasn't quite regular enough to be make it a Fivesome, but he was getting there.

"Just because you won one Jeopardy doesn't make you the undisreputable authority on everything.

"Undisreputable?" Jerry Number One said, mostly to himself.

"That doesn't sound right," Jerry Number Two said.

"Sure as hell doesn't sound right to me," Kelley joined in. He was definitely not talking to the group. He was watching *Sports Center* and drinking a Bud Light.

"The hippo can swim like forty-five miles an hour. That's how he caught the dwarf from the circus that time." Rocco was letting go.

"Little person." Jerry Number Two said. He was the closest thing to woke in the group.

"Who you calling a little person. Is that some sort of crack I have a little mind?" Rocco was beginning to amplify a bit.

"They prefer 'little person' or 'little people' to dwarf or midget," Jerry Number Two instructed.

"When did that happen?" TC said. It was his first contribution of the night.

"Around the time the hippo ate the circus midget," Jerry Number One said.

"Little person," Jerry Number Two said.

"That's right, sorry." Jerry Number One said.

"I don't think that really happened anyway," TC said.

"What?" Rocco said.

With that, the front door opened, and Trina came in. Trina was the secretary...er...admin, at the clinic where I used to work. We got close, and she always had my back in terms of covering for me when my paperwork was about to be audited. She'd tip me off or hide the worst files, so Claudia, my dreaded boss, couldn't find them.

We got close in other ways. We both went in and out of relationships, but during the times we were both out of relationships, we'd sometimes find each other. It was more than a hookup or a friend-with-benefits situation. We genuinely cared for each other. For whatever reason, we comforted each other and, to be honest, excited each other, that was for sure, but there was some sort of barrier which kept us from getting closer.

A few years ago ,she got married. That was that. I had too much respect for her to be anything more than a friend. I didn't hint at our past, didn't drop a double entendre or give her a come-hither look—whatever that means. I didn't get invited to the wedding, and I told myself it was because it was a small affair, and no one else from the clinic got invited.

I smiled from ear to ear when she came in.

She smiled, but there wasn't any happiness behind it.

"Still Pinot Grigio?" I said.

"Yeah, that's one thing that didn't change." She tried to smile, but it quickly turned into a frown.

Trina hadn't come into the bar since I took it over. She did send a congratulations and good luck card, but it wasn't lost on me she hadn't stopped by.

"You okay?" I asked.

She shrugged and her eyes welled. I knew her too well for her to pretend something wasn't going on.

She smiled a bitter smile and tears she tried not to acknowledge ran down her face.

The dogs moved toward her, Agnes first and then Al. Agnes stood directly behind her.

"Hey, 'Squal, watch the bar?" I yelled to my buddy. He worked in the business and he could handle The Foursome and Kelley.

"C'mon," It was all I said, and lead Trina through the bar upstairs to my apartment.

18

"He left," She said it as soon as she sat on the couch. She had brought her drink with her, and I poured myself a Jim Beam.

"He said he didn't feel anything for me anymore and left." She had stopped crying, like the initial disclosure was the harder part.

"When?" I asked. After I said I knew the chronology wasn't really the important thing. I should have listened.

"Sunday. I don't know if there's someone else. Probably is. Isn't there always?" She took a sip, which drained half the glass.

I shrugged. I couldn't imagine the right answer to such a question.

"Oh Duffy, I can't believe it. What am I going to do? I invested seven years with him…" It trailed off, and she started to weep hard. She held her head in her hands.

I sat next to her and put my arm around her. She turned into me so I could put both arms around her body and she buried her face into my shoulder. I could feel her cry as much as I could hear it, and her body shook.

I held her tighter. She raised her head off of my shoulder and wiped her eyes and nose with the back of her hand. There was a break in the crying.

"You've always been there. I've missed you," she said and looked it to my eyes.

"I've missed you too," I said. "You were married, and I respected that."

"You don't have to anymore."

She kissed me.

I got a rush of emotions. They were tangled, and I didn't know how to sort them out.

So, I didn't. I kissed her back. She pushed me down on the couch. Her blouse came off, and so did her bra. She unstraddled me and kicked off her ankle boots, stood up and shimmied out her stretch skin-tight jeans.

She didn't say a word. She didn't look me in the eye. She pulled my hoodie off, undid my belt, and unsnapped my jeans. She tugged at them hard and they stopped at my knee before I helped her pull them all the way down.

Then she paused to take in the sight. I was in that half-excited half…I don't know…embarrassed? feeling you get when you're so excited there's no hiding it.

She looked at it and then looked me in the eye.

"God, I've missed you. Missed this…" With that, she climbed on top of me and the two of us went at it hard.

There were the gasps, the grunts, a higher-pitched semi-shriek, and aggressive grasps at each other. Then, release.

"Oh, my God," She had slid down and placed her head on my sweaty chest. "That was awesome. I needed that. We were we always this good?"

"Remember the time in Claudia's desk chair after hours?" I said, recalling one of our first interludes.

"I remembered how it swiveled." We both giggled.

"Hard to forget," I said.

"Interesting choice of words."

I got up to refill my rocks glass and, as I stood up, I decided parading around without a stitch on felt a little uncomfortable, so I pulled on my crumpled jeans. As I did, a business card popped out of my front pocket and landed on Trina's bare stomach.

"That's a neat trick," she said. "What do you do for an encore?"

"That was the encore," I said. I thought that was pretty clever, but Trina gave me an exaggerated frown.

"Ugh, Donnie Bopp. What are you doing with this scumbag's card?" She started to hike up her jeans and threw her top over her head.

"I know Bopp. He's a little greasy, but he's alright, mostly. He helped get Ali in to a place in Florida?"

"Florida? He still doing the 'Florida shuffle?'"

"The Florida Shuffle?"

"You know how I handle the billing at the clinic? There's a thing called the Florida Shuffle because it started there. Basically, since the regulations changed, they bring patients in, usually ones who have flunked out every place else, and they exploit their Medicaid. Daily urine screens that cost eighteen dollars they bill for one fifty, exorbitant daily rates, fake referrals for PT, OT, and, of course, psychiatry."

"Isn't that the system? Shit, agencies around her do stuff like that," I said.

"Not as bad as they do. Plus, in some cases, it gets bad, I

mean really heinous. She had her clothes back on and I filled her wineglass.

"I'm afraid to ask," I said.

"They get the girls high, so their urines come back dirty. Really get them strung out. Then, they use them for prostitution right in their rehab bed. Still paying the daily rate, still paying for urines, all the extra treatment and then selling their bodies. It is horrendous."

"Bopp knows about this?" I said.

"I don't see how he couldn't." She sipped her wine. "Denial ain't just a river in Egypt."

"So, who's making the money?" I asked. Trina knew billing inside and out, but I wasn't sure understanding ownership was her strong suit.

"I don't know. It is probably on their website," she said and pulled her phone out of her jeans. The stretchy fabric covered her like spray paint, but it allowed for a phone in a pocket, which I was grateful for.

I watched Trina search the web. Her thumbs blurred, and she moved her head to give her search some body English.

"Serenity Acres...where's the 'About?'...Here it is...*Serenity Acres' mission is to improve the lives of suffering addicts through a comprehensive, systematic recovery process which treats the whole the individual, the family, and the community...*"

"The usual bullshit..." I said.

"Always the cynic," Trina paused. "Here it is. It's down at the bottom of the page by the directions. *Serenity Acres is a division of Humility, Inc.*"

"*Humility, Inc.,*" I said. "God, that's nauseating.'

"Tell me about it. Let's see what I can find on them." She got the thumbs going again. "Yeah, here's a bit more...*Humility, Inc.*

owns and operates private rehabs, outpatient clinics, sober houses, and corporate trainings encouraging a healthy and substance free lifestyle. There are facilities in ten states and Puerto Rico."

"Is there a corporate headquarters?"

"Nothing on the website?"

"Anything about looking for investors?" I asked.

"No, it is probably privately held." Trina "If that's the case, they don't really have to tell anybody anything."

"Do you get the sense they are trying to hide something?"

"No, not necessarily. A lot of companies kinda keep to themselves. If business is good, and they have a constant demand, they don't really need to drum up business."

I mulled that over.

"I'd still like to know who profits from the business. That would point towards what's going on. How could I find that out?" I said.

"Library, I suppose," Trina said.

19

Trina and I had another drink. We chatted a bit more, but after the intensity of the sex, small talk soon became awkward. We both pretended it wasn't, but it hung there like a cloud. She kissed me on the cheek.

"It was good to see you," she said and smiled. It was an inhibited smile. "Okay, if I drop in once in a while?"

That was a loaded sentence.

"I'd like that," I said.

I was uneasy. Not unhappy and there was a twinge of promise somewhere inside of me. Uneasy was the dominant emotion.

The next morning asked Billy to meet me at the University of Crawford library. I could read and was quite proud of it, but the inner workings of the library baffled me. I knew you could find out almost anything you wanted in a library, but I always sort of felt they were stingy with the information and how to access it.

Billy was in grad school and an internet the guy who could access anything. For me, there would be a learning curve, and it would be a bad use of time for me to try to learn how to get the information rather than actually getting the information.

Billy met me on the quad in front of the library. It was small for a state university and the buildings were a worn red brick. The campus was originally a mental hospital and orphanage. which was closed when atrocities perpetrated by the staff were exposed. Some said the place was haunted, and whether or not it was, the history of the buildings creeped me out.

Billy was wearing heavy grey sweats and a hoodie that said "Crawford Boxing." He carried a knapsack and a steel travel mug.

"Thanks for meeting me, especially this early," I said. It was just after eight.

"I know I'm a college student, but I'm up around five to work out and get ready for the day," he said. "What exactly are we here doing?"

"I want to find out about the business that owns the sober house Ali went to."

"That's it?" Billy looked confused.

"Yeah, why?"

Billy smiled out one side of his mouth.

"Follow me," he said and laughed a little.

The library had the smell of cleaned carpets, antiseptic spray and books. There was a smattering of students and librarian types, but there couldn't have been more than a dozen people on the first floor. There was a bank of computer monitors, metal shelves, and long, heavy wooden tables. The place had a certain element to it, and I could see why some people would be drawn to libraries. That is, until the quiet and boredom made you want to kill yourself.

Billy selected a computer in the middle of the row and motioned me to sit next to him.

"States have databases for corporations. I assume this is a Florida-based company?" He asked.

"I'd assume," I said.

I looked over his shoulder and saw he went to the Florida Department of State website. He keyed in *Serenity Acres* and *Humility, Inc...*

"Hmm, that's weird..." Billy said.

"What?" I said.

"Nothing comes up." He turned and looked at me. "Is there a chance it is incorporated in another state?"

"I dunno."

"I'll try the SEC."

"Isn't that the football conference Alabama is in. I hate Alabama," I said.

"Securities and Exchange Commission."

"Ahh, got it."

"Here it is. Not much here. Just the name. Nothing else. Could be a shell company?"

"What's that?"

"Shell companies only exist on paper. It is a way to avoid taxes by setting up a company which really has no purpose except to hold the cash. It is for tax purposes and to conceal the identities of the owners."

"Is that legal?"

"Yes, well, it can be. It can also not be."

"I don't understand.'

"If a company does it to avoid taxes, it is illegal. If they do it to be private and don't have investors or want to keep them secret, then it isn't."

"What does it say about who owns them?"

"That's just it Duff, it doesn't. That's the point."

I gave that some thought. The whole process seemed ridiculously baffling.

"Can you give me an example of a legitimate reason to form a shell company? You know, something a law-abiding, decent human would do?" I asked.

"It might be to set up financing for a startup. So, the company's sole purpose is raising capital. Or, they are avoiding foreign taxes." Billy paused to think. "People who are private. Maybe they have family who are always after them for money. Ex-wives, former business partners, former investors…maybe they are afraid of old people in their lives or they're being cautious for their own safety and welfare. Maybe someone who didn't want people to know what they are invested in or how they made their money." Billy seemed to have a handle on this.

"And what about not so law-abiding people? Why would they create a shell company?" I asked.

"That's easy. Ill-gotten money, drug money, money laundering, foreign money they don't want to pay taxes on."

"So, if Serenity Acres and Humility, Inc are owned by a shell company, what can we assume?" Now I was starting to feel like a Jack McCoy on *Law and Order*.

"Well, you can assume someone doesn't want it known they are in the drug rehab business. And if they're doing the rotten things you think they're doing, keeping their identity secret would make a lot of sense."

It sure did.

"Can you find out who owns the shell company?"

Billy hit a few more keystrokes.

"Hmm, this a little off," Billy's voice trailed off. He took a few more keystrokes.

"What? Don't leave me in the dark," I said.

"Um, the Serenity Acres/Humility, Inc are owned by a shell company registered in Florida. That makes sense and that's easy enough. But that shell company is owned by another shell company in the Cayman Islands."

"Who owns that?" I was loosely following what was going. At least I thought I did.

"That's a problem, Duff. Shell companies in the Caymans require even fewer disclosures. We can't tell anything about this shell company at all."

"So, they set up this complicated thing to hide something, right?"

"Certainly seems like it."

20

That night at the bar, it was tough for me to concentrate. Al and Agnes were out of their nook and sitting up behind Rocco and Jerry Number Two, looking at me from between the two of them. Their eyes followed me as I went back and forth cleaning glasses and absentmindedly wiping things down.

Pasquale came in holding a book, and not long after that, Kelley and TC took their places.

"What are you reading?" Jerry Number Two asked Pasquale.

"It is called *Operation Northwoods and Project Mockingbird*. It is about how our government has set up military false flag operations to serve our war interests," Pasquale said.

"False flag operations?" Rocco asked.

"You know, we make it look like we got attacked, but we really attacked ourselves," Pasquale said.

"Why the hell would we attack ourselves?" TC said. His B&B needed a refill, so I took care of it. I kept a close eye on Pasqual's Narragansett because he put them down in two sips. Kelley's Bud light was in good shape.

"We'd attack ourselves and blame it on someone country we wanted to attack but lacked justification to go after. It is how we got in Vietnam."

"C'mon, that's bullshit," Rocco said. "They shot at one of our ships."

"Actually, at first that was reported, but when it was investigated, it was clear the intelligence was off," Pasquale said.

"The intelligence was off. Sounds like this fuckin place," Kelley muttered mostly to himself.

"So LBJ decided to go with the bad intelligence and act like our ship was attacked. That gave us the so-called right to invade Vietnam and upscale our involvement there." Pasquale said.

"Why the hell would we want that?" TC asked.

"To stop communism, to fuel the military industrial complex, to broaden our colonization of the world...take your pick," Pasquale said. "False flags have been going on back to Julius Cesar's time."

"Used to love those Orange Julius shakes you'd get at the mall. What happened to them?" TC said. Rocco gave him a dirty look.

I had a question.

"So, is a false flag planned ahead of time, or is it always an opportunity like the Northwoods thing?" I said.

"The main point is to set up an action by making it appear the enemy did it, when they didn't, so you could justify attacking that entity," Pasquale said.

"Does it happen outside of the military or war situations?" Jerry Number Two said.

"Sure, all the time. You've heard of gaslighting?" Pasquale was on point and loved giving a seminar.

"Uh, maybe." TC said.

"Gaslighting is getting someone to disbelieve their own thoughts and beliefs and manipulate them into believing only the gaslighter tells the truth. For instance, someone would say news organizations are doing it. You have the conservative's networks saying everything from the left is a lie, so you have to watch them to get the truth. So, even when a network is telling the truth, it is denied because they are liberal and therefore, liars."

"My head hurts. Can we talk about sports? The Red Sox suck." Rocco said.

"I think you've hit maximum overload," I said to Pasquale.

"Yeah, I kind of figured," he said.

I checked the drinks, and everyone seemed good. A couple of dudes were at a table splitting a pitcher. A foursome of two couples feasted on wings, drinking pints. Everything seemed set.

The discussion bothered me. What about Ali? They were considering her as a suspect in the terrorist attacks against Serenity Acres. It didn't fit. Why would they want to pin it on her? What would be their motivation?

She knew the place was dirty. She knew they were working the system.

Did she know something else? Did she know more?

I had to find out.

21

When I closed the bar, I took Al and Agnes for their late evening-early morning constitutional. Neither of them had much energy, and both took the time to sniff everything around them. The problem was, for some reason, they preferred to do it at the extreme length of their 12-foot leashes. I never understood what appealed to them the most lay just out of their reach.

I guess they weren't all that much different than the rest of us.

I decided to take an inventory of what I knew and see if that pointed in a direction toward a next step.

One, I knew Ali went to Serenity Acres.

Two, I knew she left Serenity Acres after about two weeks.

Three, around that time, someone shot up the place.

Four, Ali was considered a suspect or at least a person of interest for the shooting, even though, according to Ky, she had no interest in guns, never shot again and probably wouldn't know how.

Five, the governor seemed to have a lot of energy around blaming Ali.

It felt important to list these five facts, but now that I did, it didn't point me in any particular next action. The connection to all of this was Donnie Bopp, the representative who got Ali into Serenity Arms in the first place. He was mad about losing his commission. He got weirdly distant about the tragedy which had befallen his organization. Weird, but I didn't see Bopp as a terribly deep individual. Just the opposite, he was a guy who made money, lots of money, on people's addictions and on glad-handing counselors who could refer those people.

The problem was, he spent a great deal of his time in and around Florida.

Time for a road trip? Get one of those $39 fares, rent a car, and see what I can see?

Why not?

It wasn't hard to get Billy and Pasqual to cover the bar, and Lorenzo had his eye on the gym. I checked the fares, and though they weren't the thirty-nine dollars always promised they were around seventy dollars. It was cheap enough I could afford to ask Ky to come along.

He'd be good company, knew Ali, and also knew the streets and might be able to blend in some places I'd have a harder time blending in to. I gave him a call.

"Yeah, man, I'm down. Feel like I want to be doing somethin' instead of waitin' for shit to happen. When I do that, nuthin' good is waitin' for me," he said.

He had a way around a phrase.

I gave Bopp a call to make sure this one of the weeks he'd be in Florida. There was no sense of going down there if he was up here in Crawford.

"Donnie Bopp." he answered the phone with the sort of brightness they reach in Dale Carnegie sales course.

"Donnie, it's Duff. Anything new with Ali?" I knew there wasn't, but it was an obvious reason to give him a call.

"No, Duff. I don't expect to hear from her until the authorities get her."

"You really think she was the shooter?"

"It doesn't matter what I think. Law enforcement seems to think so. If she did it, she needs to be brought to justice," he clearly had bought into the theory.

"When you up here next? I might have someone for you." I knew if I threw in a possible referral, he'd give me an honest answer.

"Hmm, Duff, can the person wait? I'm not back up north for another ten days." He sounded annoyed.

"No sweat. They're in outpatient right now and dippin' and dabblin'. Not an emergency."

"Good, I'll check in with you next week." He signed off.

Time to head to the sunshine state.

22

Ky and I landed in Sarasota at 8:15am, and immediately upon deplaning, I noticed how bright blue the sky was, how heavy and warm the air was, and how there was a pungent and sweet smell to the air. Was it palmetto? I didn't know, nor could I name any other native to Florida plants.

Ky had his ear buds in for the whole flight and even while we waited to board. I don't think I was ever around him for a period of time when he was silent for more than twenty or thirty seconds. Now, he had his dark blue hoodie in his hand, and it revealed his New York Knicks tank top.

"Thank God we made it." He exhaled it as much as he said it. "Thank God, thank God..."

"I didn't know you were afraid of flying," I said.

"I didn't know either, D. It was my first flight." He was putting his buds back in the charging case. "I also wouldn't call it fear. I don't like the word."

"What would you call it, then?" I asked.

"I was reading some shit on rational therapy. They say anxiety is irrational. That concern is a rational. I go for rational."

"Albert Ellis, huh?"

"Yessir. Some of his shit is kinda whack, but I relate."

Albert Ellis was the father of cognitive behavioral therapy. Ky never stopped amazing me.

Budget Rental gave me a silver Chevy Malibu which looked like every other car in the world. It would be good if we were going to spend our time following Bopp. We went around the roads leading out of the airport, missed the turn once, and had to go around again before we got on 41 and headed to Serenity Acres headquarters.

"Just what are we looking to find out, D?" Ky asked.

"Uh, I'm not sure. You know, in those Spenser detective books I read, he says he doesn't know until he finds it. Then we pull at it like a string until something unravels," I said.

"That shit sounds good in books. What if we find out nuthin' and just spend our time bakin' in this fuckin' sun?"

"Then I'll feel a little silly."

"Uh huh."

Google Maps directed us to the office building and, true to its promise, got us there in the seventeen minutes. It was a one-story new building in faux Spanish design at the end of a medical strip mall. There was one of those directory signs on a post out front with a list of the tenants. In addition to a chiropractor, an ophthalmologist, a massage practice, and a psychologist, the Serenity Acres sign was on top of the structure, suggesting it was the main tenant.

Donnie had his own parking space. It read "Donnie Bopp, regional representative," and it let the world know he was important enough to require his own space. It was the only vanity space, and it was occupied by a silver Lexus, the same model as the one he used up north.

We parked across from Donnie's space and down five spaces amidst the folks looking to get their backs cracked or the eyes checked.

"So, we just sit here?" Ky said.

"Yup," I said.

"This gonna mess with my ADHD, you know."

"I didn't know you had ADHD."

"I diagnosed myself."

"Always a good idea…"

Before we got into the differential diagnosis of attention disorders, Donnie did us the favor of coming out the front door and getting into his Lexus.

"Looky, looky here, there go that greasy motherfucker," Ky said.

I let him pull out, waited ten seconds and made the same turn he did out of the parking lot. I felt like a real private eye, something I knew my buddy Kelley would love to comment on.

23

I t wasn't difficult to follow Donnie. We went around Sarasota and watched him stop off at a series of sober houses. He'd go in with his briefcase, stay about fifteen minutes, and come back out and start the car and head to the next site.

The sober houses were in nice but not rich neighborhoods. If I had to describe them, I'd say they were middle class, but Florida middle class. Two had pools, but they were simple rectangular pools, not the kind built right into the house's great room. Each had a discreet "SA" above the house number.

"What's he doing?" Ky asked.

"I don't know. Maybe a daily check in to see how many residents there were. Maybe checking on the state of the house or something like that," I said.

"Shiiiit." Ky drew out the "I" sound. "Maybe he pickin' up a bundle of Benjamins from illegal activity."

"There's that," I said.

Donnie got back on 41 and headed toward Venice. TJ, my on-and-off-again, mostly off again, uh…what exactly? Let's say somewhat significant other, had grown up around Venice and spent some time covertly fighting bad guys there. I got a little bit of a twinge in the gut seeing the sign. My recent night with Trina amped the twinge a tad.

It was a twenty-minute drive to the second Venice exit. Along the Jacaranda Boulevard, I noticed the city had what seemed to be new construction. There was a new medical center, an assisted living, nursing home complex, and a gigantic Publix super market. The sun remained relentlessly bright, and it annoyed the hell out of me.

I much preferred a cold, dark, and dreary day because it was easier on the eyes, and I didn't feel the pressure to be happy. Someday, I'll talk to a shrink about that.

Donnie pulled into an old motel parking lot. It was the kind shaped like a V with two plastic chairs on the outside of each door, faux shutters on either side of the windows and a dated pool in the middle of the V. It wasn't as much run down as it was dated, and it stuck out in the pristine bright and new city of Venice. A modest rectangular sign in the front of the pool said "Ocean Crest Motel, Vacancy"

We parked across the street in yet another medical strip mall. This one featured a bone and joint office. Given the age range of the area, I'm sure business was booming.

"What the fuck he doin' here?" Ky said. "That Lexus stand out like a crack whore at the Queen of England's place."

I didn't say anything.

Donnie went to the last room on the left side of the structure.

The door opened without him knocking, and a young woman in cutoff shorts and a half t-shirt greeted him. She was barefoot. She handed him a plastic grocery bag, the kind you can't get in

New York anymore. He stood there and chatted. It didn't look like he was invited in.

A middle-aged man in just shorts appeared over the young woman's shoulder. He was white, of average build, with his hair was. He and Donnie bumped fists and then the man goosed the woman and made her jump. The man and Donnie laughed at that. Donnie might have laughed a little too much. The man grabbed her around the waist from behind and closed the door while Donnie headed back to his car, laughing.

"Don't have to be no genius to understand what's goin' on in that room,' Ky said.

"Some of it. I mean, it looks like the middle-aged guy is getting his ashes hauled by the girl. But what the hell is Donnie doing checking on it and getting a bag?" I said.

"I guessin' the bag isn't full of no health and beauty toiletries."

"No, probably not," I said.

Donnie headed back towards 41.

"What the hell do we do now?" Ky said.

"You get out and watch the motel door and see what happens. I'll follow Donnie," I said.

"I gotta stand in this heat?"

"I'll come back to get you as soon as Donnie lands some place."

Ky got out of the car, shaking his head.

"Oh man, be getting' the short end of the stick again," Ky said.

24

———

Donnie took a right on Jacaranda and headed toward Poplar, turning in a community called "Waterford." It had a gate which required a password to enter and at that point, there'd be so little traffic I was sure he would make me tailing him. So I decided to pass on by. I went back to check on Kyrone.

I tried to line up everything as I drove. This is how it seemed to stack up.

Donnie visits the sober houses and goes in and out with his briefcase. That could mean he was getting stacks of cash for something nefarious, or it could mean he was getting reports and checking on people.

The visit to the motel was different. He waited outside a door without knocking, and a young, barely clothed girl appeared with a middle-aged dude who was comfortable enough to pinch her in the ass. She responded mostly playfully. Then laughter, and a bag was handed over.

Could be a November-May romance. Could be an escort/prostitution thing. Could be a bookie Donnie bet with who had his winnings from the Dolphins game.

I tried turning it around every which way, and I came to the conclusion I didn't have every piece of the puzzle.

Kyrone had found some shade down the road from the motel under a palm tree. He was about three hundred feet from the motel. I was concerned he wouldn't have been able to see much from that vantage point.

"Man, crank up that fuckin' AC," he said when he jumped in.

"Could you keep your eye on the door from way down here?" I said. I realized it sounded a bit accusatory.

"C'mon D, give a brother some credit," he said and pursed his lips in disgust. "They left twenty minutes ago."

"Both of them?"

Ky nodded.

"A Serenity Acres minivan pulled up and waited, and the two of them came out. She was still wearing her short shorts, and he had on a velour tracksuit."

"You get a good look at them? I mean, good enough to recognize them if you saw them again?"

"For sure. The little hottie has a tattoo on her shoulder of a dragon and she got a sleeve of them up her left arm. A collage of tigers, more dragons and bears and shit."

"What about the dude?"

"Looks like a middle-aged businessman on a Saturday. Looked like every white man wearing a velour suit—out of place. Top to the suit had initials. W-M-L or W-M-T or W-N-J, you know, somethin' like that," Ky said. There was a bit of pride in his voice.

"W-M-L? W-M-T? what the hell is that?"

"I got no idea." Ky paused. "The two of them got in the van and sat in different seats, which seemed kinda whack. I mean, just been ballin' in a skanky motel and now you don't sit next to each other. Anyway, the driver was a fat brother who wore one of those skipper hats like the guy on Gilligan's Island."

"You'd recognize him again?"

"For sure. Not many brothers sportin' Gilligan Island gear. Southern brothers different than Crawford brothers."

I gave it some thought. I didn't know what to make of all of it.

"What do you think's going on?" I asked Ky.

"I think the greasy motherfucker is pimpin', and I think it is being set up by the rehab. The how's and why's, I'm not sure of."

"Me either."

25

———————

Ky and I flew back on a 6:35am Allegiant after a night in a La Quinta next to the airport. I didn't get a ton of rest between Ky's tendency to talk in his sleep and the stuff running around my head. So much of this wasn't right. We landed, and I dropped off Ky at his apartment and went home to check on the hounds and the bar.

Billy had left a note we were low on Narragansett, which didn't surprise considering Pasquale was on duty during my absence. Otherwise, the place was clean and orderly, in fact more so when I've worked the night.

Al and Agnes were sleeping when I got upstairs. Neither of them immediately raised their head and charged me like I was one of those returning soldiers you see in an internet video. Billy probably had walked them, and knowing him, it was a good, long walk. When I threw my keys down on the table, Al let out a low volume half growl but tucked his head back into his body and resumed sleep. It was close to opening, and I didn't know what else to do, so I headed downstairs to get ready for the day.

CNN was breaking down a debate between the Florida and California governors.

"Sir, would you or would you not support an across the board ban on abortion?" The California governor turned towards his opponent with squared shoulder and a forceful look. I was sure he had been instructed on every aspect of body language and voice control by a series of experts.

"I have and always will support the sanctity of life, sir." The Floridian said. He put in as much sanctimony into his tone as humanly possible.

"Answer the question!" Governor Cali came back with.

"I just did, sir!" The Floridian's eyes got beadier, and he held his glance as he turned toward Mr. California a beat or two longer than what was required. It was, I presume, it was supposed to show he was not intimidated, and he was probably ready to open up a can of Christian fundamentalist whoop ass on him at any moment.

Put either of them in the ring with one of my novice teenage boxers from the Y, and after they took their first body shot, both of them would puke for a week. It reminded me real life fighters rarely had chest puffing interactions like this because they didn't need to. They knew they could fight, and they knew what was bluster. It didn't mean they knew they'd win every fight, but they had enough understanding of what real fighting was that they didn't have to fake it.

This interaction with two fighters would've gone like this.

California Governor: "Hey, would you ban abortion?"

Florida Governor: "Yup."

California Governor: "That's fucked up."

Florida Governor: {Shrug}

California Governor: {Shrug}

You disagree and you move on. If things were truly to escalate, one governor would go over to the other governor and punch him. The other one would block it or counter it or whatever. It would be a fight. Then it would be over.

Real fighters don't bluster. They don't have to. It is a waste of time and means absolutely nothing to the outcome. They don't start a fight with an insult, then a counter-insult, then a shove, then a punch. If there's a fight, it is on, and it is time to get busy.

These two blowhards could bluster endlessly.

It was why I preferred boxing gyms.

The iPhone did its digital thing which took the place of the ring, and I saw it was Trace.

"Duff, I got something for you," he said.

"Yeah?" I said.

"I got to see the video of the sober house shooting, and there's something interesting."

"Yeah?"

"You said your girl, I think her name was Ali, was a little, light-skinned African American, right?"

"Yeah, that's right."

"She have a large tattoo of a heart on the back of her right hand?"

"No."

"You're sure?"

"Yeah, I used to see her every day. She didn't have a tattoo on the back of her hand."

"It only flashes for a second, and they had to enlarge it and slow it down and, all the shit forensics can do, but there's definitely a hear tattoo of her right hand."

"She didn't have one," I said.

"Then, she's not the shooter."

26

The two o'clock group was in right on time at two seventeen. Carl had on a crew neck Kelly green sweater, khakis, and tasseled loafers. Kay had on a beige oversized sweatshirt with a hoodie and sported those Yezzi rubber shoes. Ky had on his loose-fitting jeans and Knicks hoodie. Juan had his Carhartt jacket on and a Yankees cap.

"I've been hearing on the news Ali is a person of interest in that shooting," Kay said.

"She may be, but it's bullshit," Ky said.

"I don't see her as a gun person," Carl said.

"Her, no way," Juan said.

They looked at me like I might have an explanation. I didn't. I shrugged.

"All of this is around addiction," Kay said.

"How so," Juan said.

"If Ali wasn't using and addicted and fucked up, she wouldn't be in Florida getting help, she wouldn't be in a fucked up place, and she wouldn't have had to run away," Kay said.

"More things in life fuck things up than drugs and alcohol," Juan said, and sipped his coffee.

"D, do you sometimes think addicts somehow think they are…I don't know…like special? Like we have a built in…I don't know…excuse for everything? Is it we are all so self-centered?" Ky said.

I didn't want to field that and turned it back to them.

"I don't know. What do you all think?" I said.

"I think it is what we got, and it causes problems. But I think Ky is right. It isn't the only problem out there. And if all you do is hang around with recovering people, I can see where it can become like an 'Us against the world'" Carl said.

"You mean, like, because some addicts isolate themselves and only hang with other addicts, that's all they see and hear?" Juan asked.

"And then it makes us like victims and outside normal people," Kay said.

"Who's normal?" Carl said.

"You know what I mean," Kay said.

"I think that's the point we're all getting at. All of us, all people get disturbed by things. Just because we're addicts doesn't make us different. We just use more than others," Carl said.

"And other folks do other shit to deal," Juan said. "Maybe that shit doesn't get them into as much trouble, but it doesn't make them healthier."

"This is making my hair hurt," Kay said.

That got a laugh from the group.

Rocco came in, and as he always did, gave the group and me a cursory wave to not disturb us. He moved down the bar, grabbed the remote and put on Fox News. He set the volume low out of respect for the group.

"Anyway, Ali is responsible for the trouble she's in, no doubt," Ky said.

"I dunno, man. I dunno if that girl ever had much of a chance not to be an addict. Didn't you tell me her mom is a crackhead and had her at fourteen?" Juan said.

"She still responsible, right, D?" Ky said.

I hesitated. It didn't seem like an easy answer. "Um, maybe, I'd put it this way. If…"

Ky interrupted. "Yo, Yo, Yo, Mr. Rocco, please turn that up. Please give that some volume!"

It startled Rocco, but he turned it up.

A teased blond Fox reporter was interviewing the governor of Florida.

"That's him, D. That's him!" Ky said.

I turned toward the TV.

"That's him! That's the dude!" Ky said.

"The governor of Florida?" I said.

"He was the dude at the motel! He was the one with that greasy motherfucker Bopp and the girl."

I looked at the TV and I looked back at Ky.

"C'mon Ky…"

"Sure as I was born," He watched the TV. "Holy fuckin' shit."

"C'mon, you're seeing shit," I said.

"I'm telling you that's him," Ky said as he stared at the TV.

"The governor of Florida is the guy you saw in the motel? No…"

Ky didn't move his eyes from the television. He kept muttering something to himself. It was hard to make out with

Fox news in the background. I stepped closer to Ky to make out what he was saying. It got clearer.

"Holy fuckin' shit...Holy fuckin shit..." he kept saying.

"Holy fuckin' shit is right," I thought.

27

I needed to talk to Kelley, and I prayed he had the day shift today and he would drop by the bar tonight. The Foursome and Pasquale were in, plus a couple from the neighborhood who came in to eat. This had been about their third time in, and they were nice. The guy was simple. He ordered wings and chips, preferred them with a Korean sauce, and he liked extra carrots and celery. His wife, who was beautiful, announced on the first night she was vegetarian, which made Rocco's head spin around and his eyes to rolling. She ordered a Rueben without the meat. Her name was Sue and together we dubbed the sandwich the Sueben.

Tonight, she asked for a BLT without bacon. She asked if I could substitute cheese for the bacon and add spicy mustard. Rocco stared at her.

I told her that her CLT would be right up. She clapped. Rocco raised his eyebrows in an exaggerated way and looked at me as I headed to the counter by the grill to make my masterpiece.

Kelley came in as the couple was finishing their dinner.

I slid the Bud Light in front of him.

"Can I ask you something?" I said.

"You just did," He said, and drank from the longneck.

"Me and Ky went to Florida a couple of days ago and followed that guy Donnie around. We saw him make stops at sober houses. Then he went to a shady motel where we saw him talk to what looked like a guy with a hooker."

I was going fast on purpose because I didn't want him to tell me I was an asshole until I got it all out. "Then last night when Ky saw the Florida governor on the news, he knew it was the guy with the hooker."

Kelley took another long pull on the Bud Light.

He put it down on the bar slowly and methodically. Yet he didn't say anything. He just glared at me. Then, he raised the bottle to his mouth again and took another sip and slowly put it back down. He continued to glare at me.

"I don't even know what the stupidest part is of all the shit you vomited out at me." He shook his head. "Maybe it is a spontaneous trip to Florida with your friend, the recovering guy from the clinic—that in itself is something else. Or, maybe it is putting surveillance on a guy who represents clinics going to clinics—that's a hot clue…"

I felt myself start to deflate a bit. But I couldn't stop him. I brought this on myself. He continued.

"I also like spying on a guy who may or may not have been with a paid sex worker, that's what we call them now, who was out getting his ashes hauled on a weekday and not really bothering anyone…"

"Kell…" he wouldn't let me finish.

"But the cherry on top of this is your new best friend Ky, who has spent most of his life on the street doing drugs has now, after the fact, identified the ash haulee as the governor of the great state of Florida, and, I might add, a presidential candidate."

"Kell, I—"

TC interrupted.

"Would the guy be the ash haulee, or would that be the hooker?"

"You know, TC, I'm not sure. Let's kick it around a little." Kelley never engaged the Foursome. "Rocco, what do you think?"

"The hooker would be the haulee. She's the one doing all the work, ain't she?"

"Hmm, I believe it could go either way," Kelley said, keeping it going. "Jerry Number One?"

"Huh?" Jerry was watching Wheel of Fortune. "I'm trying to solve."

"Okay, we can come back to you. Pasquale?"

Pasquale took a dramatic pull from the Narragansett.

"I believe, detective, that the customer is the haulee in he is the one being, how we could say, serviced. As the euphemism goes, he is the one whose ashes, as we say, are being addressed. Vis-à-vis, he is the haulee." He hit his knuckles on the bar like a supreme court judge making a decision.

"I think we have our last word," Thank you Mr. P.

With that, Kelley finished his beer and left.

28

———

"She called again," Ky said as he came into the bar for his second visit of the day. He crossed paths with Kelley as the detective headed out of the bar.

"What?" I said. I think my frustration was easy to read.

"She's in Pittsfield. I think she was high." Ky didn't really care about my frustration.

"Shit." In all of this mess, I had forgotten about her recovery. "What did she tell you?"

"She was high as hell and barely making sense. Said she couldn't talk on the phone, they'd be listening. Said I had to come help her." Ky was breathing hard and his eyes were darting around the room.

"Who is the 'they' she was talking about?"

"Shit, D, I told you she was high as could be. She wasn't making no sense. Talkin' about getting' out of there, and she wasn't no whore."

"You know where she is in Pittsfield?"

"I'm guessin' her mother's. C'mon D, we gotta go get her. I think she's in trouble."

I took a deep breath and motioned to Ky with my hands out palms up, silently asking him to chill out. I tried to think.

"Duff, I'm goin' whether you go with me or not." Ky folded his arms in defiance.

I took another deep breath. I looked down the bar.

"Hey 'Squal?" He looked up from his book, took a sip of Narragansett. "Can you watch the bar again?"

He nodded without saying anything. He got up and went behind the bar. I grabbed my coat, walked around the bar, slapped 'Squale on the back, and got my car keys out. We were off.

A half an hour into the trip, we were crossing into Massachusetts, and the phone went off. It came up Venice, Florida and I felt it in my gut.

"You gonna answer that?" Ky said.

I got it on the fifth ring before it went to voice mail.

"This is Duffy."

"Duff, it is TJ." She didn't say anything after that. The pause was chilling. She had left without any explanation after we had, um, I guess, a relationship. She'd randomly sent an email once in a while. There was no closure to what we had. Sometimes she seemed to suggest she still wanted something with me. It was all enough to keep me hanging and filled with anxiety. To say my feelings were complicated was an understatement.

"Hey, what's up?" I had that distant feeling I get where I kind of feel outside of myself and can hear my own voice.

"Um, this is weird. I know I haven't been in touch, so I was hesitant to reach out." She paused again, and I waited. "Um, I'm working on a human trafficking task force. Something came up, and I thought of you."

She wasn't calling because she missed me, couldn't live without me, and was coming back. She was looking for a favor.

"Yeah?" I said. It sounded a bit more pissy than I wanted it to.

"That thing in Sarasota, the rehab terrorism thing? There seems to have been a trafficking aspect to it."

"Meaning?"

"The women in the place are addicts. They take them in and exploit their benefits. There's also evidence they deal them drugs or even are a hub for dealing drugs."

"The Florida Shuffle, right?"

"Yeah, but it goes further here. They keep the girls addicted and make them into sex workers to get their drugs. They continue to exploit their insurance benefits, keep them high to make sure their urines come back dirty and then make them trick."

I swallowed.

"I saw that girl who split was from Crawford. She's a person of interest and she's missing. We can't find her. I figured it had to do with drugs and was in Crawford. Thought you might be connected."

My mind raced. So much was wrapped up with TJ, it was tough to keep things straight. I didn't like Ali being a person of interest, and all that shit the governor was saying on the news. I didn't think Ky could possibly be right when he identified the man at the motel. But something felt wrong, and I didn't want to put Ali in danger.

I went with my instinct. It wasn't always the best move.

"I don't know anything about it." I heard come out of my mouth.

29

———

I got quiet after the call ended. Ky was quiet too.

It seemed like it was quiet for a long time, and we were about ten minutes outside Pittsfield.

"That was her, huh?" Ky broke the silence.

"What do you mean?" I said.

"C'mon D. You told me about that one who left. That was her, right?"

Ky was a tough guy to bullshit.

"Yeah."

"I could tell. A man gets a certain way when he hears from the one."

I thought that over. I was going to argue the point, but I decided against it. Instead, I let it get quiet again and we pulled into Pittsfield.

"The one?" Does "The One" leave without explanation? Does "The One" not stay in contact? Does "The One" continually fuck with your emotions?

A light snow was falling, and in the streetlights, it didn't make Pittsfield look any prettier. It made it look angry and grey.

We headed up the hill where Ali's mom lived. The flurries began to cover the litter, but they hadn't just yet. When it piled up, it might make the city look more tidy, but now snow underlined the half-covered garbage and brought more attention to it.

It was too cold for her to be sitting on her stoop. That's what the change of seasons did in the ghetto. It brought people inside, isolated them more, and I think that's when getting high got worse. Hot nights where everyone escaped outside may bring more crime and aggression, but the cold brought more heartbreak.

"We gotta rap on the door," Ky said. The porch had no safety light, none of the houses on the block did. It was like they didn't want to make the pretension it would keep anyone safe.

"Go ahead," I said.

Ky knocked on the door with the four knuckles of his right hand. The door was ajar and opened about a half a foot.

He looked back as if to ask if he should go in.

I nodded.

Ky slowly opened the door with his shoulder. He looked back at me and moved closer. He wiped his hand down the left side of the door frame in what I assumed was a motion to find a light switch. He didn't find one.

"Yo, anyone home?" He called out.

No one answered.

"Yo, anyone home?" Ky increased the volume in his voice.

I scrolled on the flashlight of my iPhone. It illuminated about four feet in front of us. There was a Keystone light can on the floor next to some wadded-up paper towel and a crumpled MacDonald's bag. Even in the low light, I could tell the place was a mess.

We inched forward and got to a threshold leading into the

kitchen. Dishes filled the sink, and the garbage can had spilled over. Empty Styrofoam containers littered the floor. A door to the side of the kitchen was half open, and Ky moved toward it.

I shone my phone in his direction to give him some light, but it wasn't powerful enough. I moved closer as Ky quietly pushed the door open. It appeared to be a bedroom.

"Yo, anyone home?" He stepped into the room and flicked on the light. "Of fuck…"

I stepped into the room behind Ky, but I had a good idea what I was about to see.

Ali's mom was on her back, fully clothed in her ripped sweats and men's t-shirt. She was barefoot.

And there was a bullet hole in the middle of her forehead.

30

"Let's get the hell out of here," I said.

"Fuck yeah," Ky said.

I should have called the police. I should have waited, but something told me there wasn't any time to waste. Something inside me told me to get the hell out of there.

We ran down the dilapidated steps. Me first and Ky right behind me. When we hit the sidewalk, a volley of gunshots rang out. It only took me a moment to realize they were aimed at us.

"Holy fuckin' shit!" Ky shouted.

"To the car! Stay low, stay around the parked cars along the street." I yelled.

Another burst of fire smashed two windshields along the street. The El Dorado was another fifty feet down the hill. I jumped to the ground and bear-crawled the rest of the way.

"Get in on my side!" I yelled to Ky. He awkwardly climbed over me and ducked down under the window. In the distance, I heard sirens.

God bless General Motors and the work they did in the seventies. The El Dorado started up right away. I hit the gas and all eight cylinders fired up. It took just a block to hit seventy, and I almost lost control, making the hard left, but I straightened her out and was at eighty when I hit the entrance to the turnpike.

"Holy fuckin shit..." Ky said, but with less terror in his voice.

I slowed to enter the turnpike, but I did so nervously. Once on the highway, the car got back to 85, and we had the right lane all to ourselves as far as I could see.

"The shots stopped," Ky said as much to himself as to me.

I looked in my rearview.

"I don't think there's anyone following us," I said.

"Holy shit, D. What the hell does this have to do with recovery?"

We both got a laugh at that.

"Something about keeping it simple, I think," I said.

"Word, man, fucking word."

My breathing began to slow, but I had that buzzing in my chest you get after trauma. It had something to do with the fight-or-flight mechanism, but seldom in life is it literally a life and death situation. I wish in my life it happened less. I had more than my share of it, and despite what action movies depicted, there wasn't anything fun about it.

"Who knew we were going to Pittsfield?" Ky asked.

"How could anyone know? We decided on a whim two hours ago," I said.

"Then someone was watching the house."

I gave it some thought.

"Somebody kills Ali's mom, then waits around to shoot at anyone who comes?" It didn't make any sense.

"So, someone's camping out watchin.'" It wasn't a question.

"Why?" I asked.

"Yeah, why kill a dried-up old crackhead?"

"She must have got something somebody wants," Ky said. "Maybe they thought Ali would show. Or she knows something somebody don't want her to know—or probably more importantly somebody else to know."

I gave that some thought.

We were coming up to one of the last Massachusetts exits. We were both chewing on what had happened and doing our best to make sense of it. Ky shocked me out of my reverie.

"Holy shit! Holy fuckin' shit!" Ky yelled. It startled the hell out of me.

"What? Man, easy. You're gonna make me run off the road."

"Back there, D. Back there, that sign!" He couldn't contain himself.

"Huh?"

"That sign! That damn sign before the exit."

"Calm down, man. You're not making any sense."

Ky exhaled hard.

"The sign was one of those signs coming up to the exits. It tells you what's up ahead," Ky said.

"So?"

"It said Western New Massachusetts Law School."

"Yeah, and?" It was starting to piss me off.

"The logo, D. The damn logo."

"What about it?"

"It was on the sweat suit on the guy in the motel." Ky said.

"Huh?"

"The fuckin' governor."

31

———

"You sure about this?" I asked Ky. My head was spinning.

"Yeah, D. C'mon man, that logo stands out. It was what he was wearing, for sure," Ky said.

We were in New York and would be home in about twenty minutes. I couldn't wait. I had to know.

"Look him up on the internet," I said.

"You got it."

Ky took out his phone and typed rapidly with his thumbs. Ky did that thing where he skimmed the page out loud. He was mostly talking to himself, tracking the information.

"Forty-five years old...governor since 2019...Republican... former representative...United States Army...lieutenant...Iraq War...Silver Star...undergraduate degree...Florida State...law degree..."

"Florida State," Ky said flatly.

I didn't say anything for a long time. I didn't want to pile on and make Ky feel like he was stupid.

"Why the fuck would he be wearing the gear of another law school?" Ky said.

I had to say it.

"Look, Ky, you really think the governor, a president wanna-be, is the guy you saw? C'mon man…" I said.

"Oh, because I'm an addict, I see crazy shit? Ghetto crackhead makin' shit up?"

"I never said that." I felt awful.

We hit the Crawford city limits. We'd be at the bar in five minutes.

I pulled into the parking spot in front of the bar. Ky let out a long breath and said he was headed home.

The bar was just the Foursome and Pasquale. Pasquale was arguing with Rocco. I went behind the bar and poured myself a bourbon. It was probably around four fingers. My heart rate was still up, and I was trying to bring it down.

"The FBI and the CIA are totally different organizations. They barely speak to each other. That's the problem," Pasquale said.

"They are divisions under Homeland Security. They all fit together," Rocco countered.

"I'm telling you, that's the problem. They don't all fit together."

"Don't they all do the same thing, anyway?" TC said.

"No, they have distinct areas without much overlap. For instance, you know the FBI spends more time chasing white collar shit with accountants. They go after shit like money laundering," Pasquale said.

"I still think they work together." Rocco wouldn't let go.

"Homeland security does some financial forensic stuff, too. Following terrorists and their funding," Pasquale said.

Something struck me.

"Say that again, 'Squal?"

"Say what…"

"The Homeland Security and forensic financial accounting thing."

"Everybody thinks these agencies are all spy and special forces shit. So much of what they do is tracking financial stuff like money laundering."

"Money laundering…like off-shore accounts…shell companies and that shit?"

"Yes, exactly."

It was time to call TJ.

32

Pasquale was willing to keep watching the bar. I headed up to the apartment to call TJ.

I took in a breath of air. Calling her scared me whether I wanted to admit it or not. This wasn't about our relationship.

"I lied to you before when I said I hadn't heard from Ali," I said as soon as she answered.

She was quiet for more than a moment of thought.

"Ok, I'm not sure why. I mean, I know you don't owe me anything, and I can understand that—" I didn't let her finish.

"It had nothing to do with that."

Again, the lengthy silence.

"Ok, what did it have to do with?"

This time, it was my turn to be quiet. I wasn't sure why I lied to her.

"Um, we were in the middle of, uh, doing something and I didn't want to complicate anything in the moment."

"Duffy, you're not in law enforcement. What the hell are you doing? I mean, I don't want to get judgmental but, damn."

It pissed me off. She was right, but it pissed me off.

"Well, we all have our faults, I guess," I said.

"What's that supposed to mean?" She said.

I knew it was a passive aggressive thing to say. I prided myself on being direct, but when things were this emotional, I wasn't at my best.

"Yeah, that was passive aggressive. I'll own that. And this might be some sort of official business and all but look, you've taken off on me, cut things off without an explanation, more than once. You want me to be direct? Yeah, that pisses me off."

It got really quiet. Longer than the last couple of times.

"I deserve that," she said.

"Fuck yeah, you do."

"Look, I own it. You don't have to pile on, alright?"

My turn to be quiet. When you spend such a long time pushing something down, not talking about, not letting yourself feel about, when you scratch the itch of letting it shake loose, it can be tough to rein it in.

"Been a long time…" I said.

"I don't know what else to say, except I'm sorry," she said.

Quiet.

"Um, yeah. Might take me a bit to let that sink in."

Quiet.

"Let's switch gears. We heard from Ali. Heard she might be in Pittsfield with her mother. We went there, found her mother dead. We got out of there and got shot at." I said it all as concisely as I could.

"You call the cops? Anything like that?"

"No."

"Why the hell not? Geez, you're in over your head."

I gave it some thought. I had some crazy shit running around my head.

"Alright, here goes. You can laugh at this if you want." I gathered myself. "My friend, the guy who knows Ali, thinks he saw the governor coming out of a sleazy motel with one of the Serenity Acres residents. Ali had no history of violence, no history of using a gun, and went there to get help. I don't know. I just don't know…"

"You think the governor of Florida is behind something?"

"I don't know. But if he is, in the meantime, I'm not sure I can trust law enforcement. I don't know who are the good guys. I don't like how the governor jumped on the idea she was, what do they call it, a 'person of interest?'" It makes no sense.

"What would be his motivation?"

"I have no idea." I stopped for a second. "And why are you involved in this? Is this a Homeland Security thing?"

"Some parts of it have to do with human trafficking,"

"I know about the Florida Shuffle. What has the good governor done about that in his fine state?"

TJ didn't say anything.

I was worn out. I didn't like the out of control feeling. I hadn't talked to her in a year and lived with her in and out of mind. The personal blending with this other shit was too much.

"I gotta go." I signed off.

33

———

When I got back down to the bar, the Foursome had left and Kelley was there.

"Am I off duty now?" Pasquale said.

"Yeah, man. Thanks for the help," I said. He grabbed a Narragansett and headed back to the customer side of the bar.

"Good evening detective," I said to Kelley. We got in arguments, but when they were over, they were over.

"What happened in Pittsfield? Anything exciting?" You could cut the sarcasm with a knife. "Actually, don't tell me."

"Okay…" I said.

"I guess a semi-street person was shot in the forehead in her ghetto house. I also heard some shots were fired on the street in front of her place. But I'm guessing you wouldn't know about that."

I didn't say anything.

"You know withholding information in a murder case is a felony?"

I kept my mouth shut.

"One of these days, Duff, shit isn't going to come out okay, you know. I don't have any friends in Pittsfield. You're on your own this time."

I nodded.

"Good luck."

He finished his beer and left. He was right, of course. He was always right. I didn't like to hear it.

"Duff, I'm heading out. I told them I'd help with closing at The Taco," Pasquale said.

"Hey—thanks for the help. I appreciate it.

He shot me a wink and headed out, but as he was going through the threshold Trina came in.

It was turning into a complicated evening for me.

"Just me?" she said with a smile. It was a great smile.

"Quality over quantity when it comes to company." I poured her a Pinot Grigio. "You're out late."

"My son's at my mom's. I couldn't sleep."

I felt a twinge of something in my gut. Excitement? Possibility? It probably wasn't the healthiest thing with TJ on the mind, but it would be effective in getting her off my mind.

"Any news on Ali?" she asked.

"Yeah, Ky said he heard from her and she's in Pittsfield, her hometown. We went over there but couldn't find her." I left out the part about the murder.

"You went to Florida too?"

"How'd you know about that?"

"I stopped in when you were gone." That was interesting, but I tried not to show any reaction. "What did you find out?"

"I don't know except Ky thought he saw the governor coming out of sleazy motel with one of the girls and Bopp. They got into a Serenity Acres mini-van and sped away. I didn't see it. Ky did."

"The governor? Really?"

"Yeah, and get this, Ky swears he was wearing a Western Massachusetts warm up."

"Makes sense. He went there, at least for a year."

"What? He went to FSU for law school."

"His degree is from Florida State, but he went to WME first. Yeah, there was an article about it earlier in the year when they were speculating on candidates."

"Pittsfield is Ali's birthplace..."

"A coincidence?" Trina said.

"I hate coincidences." I said.

34

"It could be a coincidence, couldn't it?" Trina.

"Of course, it could be but it feels weird, doesn't it?" I said.

Trina mulled that over. She had this way of tilting her to the left when she pondered something. It gave me a chance to look at her. Her dark brown hair cut in a bob, the black turtleneck, dark blue stretch jeans and ankle boots which showed a little ankle before the cuff of the jeans.

"I guess it does feel weird," she said.

I went behind the bar to fill her wineglass and while there got myself a bourbon.

I brought the glasses around the bar and sat. I offered a clink of a toast.

"Duff, we've known each other for a long time," she said.

"Twenty years, right?"

"Something like that."

She pondered again. It made me stir.

"We haven't just been friends with benefits all this time, have we?" she said.

"Oh God, no."

More pondering.

"Then what have we've been?"

I swallowed. I sipped the Beam, partly for time, which I didn't want to take too much of.

"Hmm…is it something we have to define?"

"Not a 'have to' and not something I want you to feel pressured about. It's only we, well, we aren't in our early twenties anymore."

"That's for sure." She was looking at me, and she waited. I drank, looked straight ahead, and prayed I'd say the right thing.

"You've been there for me whenever I needed you," I said and looked at her.

"You've been there for me too," she said. "Why were there gaps where we stayed away?"

I didn't have a good answer for that. This was Trina, and I didn't want to ever be dishonest with her.

"Life got in the way. I don't mean to be flip or cliché. I'm not the most together guy. Sometimes, I still feel like I have to figure out how to live, and I don't know what to do. I still live on instinct and impulse a lot of the time. I mean, look at this place. What the hell am I doing here?"

She waited a beat or two. Then she put her hand on my forearm and waited for me to look at her.

"I think you're the most together man I know."

"Ha! That's a good one…"

"I don't know if 'having it together means' always feeling good or certain or confident. I think it might mean being real. Having standards that are important to keep and doing everything you can to keep them. You do that." She kept looking at me.

"I don't feel together…"

She kissed me. She left a hand gently on my chest and lightly held my head in her other hand. It was a tender kiss at first. It turned into a passionate one before long. I stood and lifted her off her bar stool. With my back to the bar held her tightly and kissed her deeply.

Her hand found its way under my shirt and she untucked her turtleneck. I had my hands on the small of her back and she leaned into me.

She put both hands on my chest and lightly pushed off of me.

"Can we go upstairs?" She said.

"Yes," I said.

35

It was even more intense than last time.

Afterward we laid in bed, slowing our breathing with me on my back and Trina resting her head on my chest. We didn't say anything.

Then, I noticed she was crying softly. I stroked her hair and thought about whether I should say anything. Sometimes it helped and comforted someone, and sometimes it seemed like an invasion. Still, saying nothing seemed insensitive.

"You okay?" I said.

Trina nodded and sniffed and then awkwardly wiped at her nose before putting her head back down. She didn't want to speak.

I was never quite comfortable with silence, but as I've gotten older, I recognized not everyone is able to emote on the spot. Trina must have had some complex emotions going and crying seemed pretty appropriate.

My phone rang.

"Go ahead, it's ok," Trina said. She got out of bed and started to get dressed.

It was Ky. I held a finger at Trina, motioning I wanted her to stay. She shook her head and continued to wiggle into her jeans.

"She called. She's out of Pittsfield. She say she know her mom is dead. She say she has an idea who did it," Ky said. He was speaking in a staccato cadence, almost talking in short bursts.

"Who does she think did it?" I said.

"Wouldn't say."

"Aw c'mon man. Why not?"

"She say she don't trust the telephone line. That she don't trust nothing."

"What else?"

"Nothing. After that, she said she had to go and hung up."

"Do we know where she is or where she's going?"

"Nope. I don't know shit."

Trina had dressed, blew me a kiss, and headed out.

"Man, I'm not sure where this leaves us," I said.

"Duff..." Ky hesitated. "How she know her mom was killed?"

"I don't think it made the news."

"That's right. I searched the internet and all the TV stations. Ain't nothing about no killing in Pittsfield."

I gave it some thought.

"Then she had to have been there or seen or know someone who did," I said.

"It was me and you and whoever killed her and whoever shot at us...which could be the same."

"Maybe she went to see her mom and walked up on it like me and you," I said.

"Why wouldn't she stick around or call five-o?"

"Same reason me and you got the hell out of there."

"So, she knows someone is after her, and she know they willing to kill her." Ky quickened his pace, almost like he knew something.

"Yeah…" I said. "The Serenity Acres people?"

"Why exactly would they want her dead?" Ky was employing the Socratic method as much as he was asking to find out.

"Because she know something they don't want her to know."

"Uh-huh. Like maybe a governor is into some bad shit." Ky said. "Why else do people get killed?"

"Sex and money," I said.

"Uh-huh." Ky said. "D, you know what we gotta do?"

"What?"

"Find out more about the money." Ky said.

He was right.

36

Follow the money. It was a cliché, of course, but clichés get repeated for a reason—they are often true, or at least sort of true.

The problem was following the money in this case was next to impossible. One shell company wrapped in another offshore, and no way an average guy could research it. That concept gave me some pause.

If an average guy couldn't, who could?

My buddy Trace worked for the CIA. Sure, he was in the psychology department doing research, and he counseled agents, but he was on the periphery of things and might be hip to the chatter. Shit, I thought, I'm even starting to think like I was a super spy. I mean, who uses "chatter?"

It was 9:45 in the morning, and if Trace was in Albany, he'd be like me and be setting up the tavern for the day. Maybe I should say I was supposed to be setting up the bar. Right now, I was late finishing up feeding Al and Agnes. I gave Trace a call.

"Hey Duff, what's up?"

"Can I ask you another spy question? It is okay to say no if I'm wearing out my welcome," I said.

"I'll tell you what I can. If it means breaching something I'm not supposed to talk about, then I can't talk about it."

"That's fair enough. I know you're studying mass shootings lately, and I know that means you are on the fringes of the Serenity Acres thing."

"Yeah, go on…"

"I looked in to the ownership of the company, and it got weird."

"Weird?"

"It is owned by a shell company, and that shell company is owned by another shell company, offshore, in the Cayman Islands. Do you guys know about that or even care about that?"

"I know for sure I don't know anything about that. I don't think it is an angle we care about. In fact, I'm not sure why you'd be concerned about it. Clue me in."

I took in some air and tried to organize my thoughts so I didn't sound like a crazy conspiracy nut on talk radio.

"Okay, here goes. You and I have talked about the Florida Shuffle. If Ali was getting manipulated and abused in that place, it is likely she split. That kid has no history of violence or gun use, so it makes zero sense to me she would all of a sudden pull a Columbine on the place."

"Okay…go on." I got the impression Trace was listening.

"So, suppose she's getting set up or framed. Why would someone do that? Usually, it would have to be she knew something and that something could cause damage to someone's money or power."

"Yeah…like who?" Trace was beginning to sound skeptical.

"The governor went to law school for a year in Ali's

hometown. We think we saw him coming out of a sleazy hotel with a young girl and getting chauffeured around in a Serenity Acres minivan."

"Okay...cut to the chase. Are you saying the governor of Florida, the guy who wants to be the next president, is setting up your friend because, um, she knows something that could either cost him his money or his power?"

"Or his chance at power." I said.

"You started this with a 'follow the money' scenario."

"Yeah, how could the governor be profiting from the place?"

"You got me there, Duff. He's getting payments? He's selling women? Help me out here."

"Maybe he owns the place." I said.

The line went silent.

"Own Serenity Acres? Why would he keep that a secret?" The skepticism was back in his voice.

"Because he's running a Florida Shuffle and trafficking the girls he keeps addicted."

"That's a lot to unpack, D."

"How do I find out about the shell company?"

"Not up our alley. FBI does that kind of shit for tax evasion. Homeland Security does it when it involves funding terrorism and stuff like that."

"Would they do it for something that has to do with human trafficking?"

"Sure, if it was pertinent."

"They would?"

"Yeah, I'm sure they would."

I signed off with Trace. I needed to talk to someone else.

37

TJ didn't answer, and I was relieved.

Seeking her out wasn't something I ever took lightly. She tended to provoke strong feelings inside of me, and mostly they were feelings of a lack of control. There was a time when the feelings were intensely positive, and, strangely, they were challenging to handle as well.

"If you can, get your forensic accountants to find out who owns Serenity Acres or actually who owns the shell companies that own Serenity Acres." I said into her voice message. I felt a bit cowardly not talking to her, but I also was happy I didn't have to hear her voice or decide on what else to say to her.

I opened the bar and set up. I had to restock the Narragansett and order some more. We needed a few bottles of Pinot Grigio, and I realized it was because Trina stopped by more and more regularly. We were good with TC's B & B, and I didn't have to order any Dewar's yet for Rocco. I ordered some Boom Sauce in case Trace stopped by and completed the order with some napkins, straws, and swizzle sticks.

My phone pinged with a reminder the lawyer was stopping

in today to review some details of the probate or something which had to do with AJ leaving the bar to me. AJ was the previous owner who died suddenly and surprised the hell out of me by leaving me the bar. I didn't know whether to bless him or curse him for that action.

The appointment was for 10 am before the bar opened. Fowler, the lawyer, never got to the point of any of his stories, usually forgot something, or didn't know exactly what he was supposed to do. Today's appointment was because he didn't get my signature on something last year when the bar transferred to me. He was my court-appointed attorney when I got jammed up in Las Vegas awhile back, and I got out of the trouble. He may take credit for getting me released, but he really had nothing to do with it. If I had relied on him, I'm sure I'd be doing life.

It was 10:25 when he came in.

"Mr. Dombrowski," he said, offering his hand. "Good to see you again."

"What's with the hair?" I was distracted by the fact he now had a shaved head. For some reason, it made his broken nose more pronounced.

"Well, you know, it was either doing a first-to-third comb over or, well, this," he sort of shrugged when he said. He took off the long overcoat and draped it on a bar stool. He took a seat.

"How do you take your coffee?" I asked. I poured a black cup for me into my "You wouldn't understand, it's a Basset Thing!" my old friend Shelly sent me.

"Black is fine," Fowler said.

"Hey, why don't you drop the Mr. Dombrowski thing and call me Duff. We've known each other for a while now."

"Okay, Duff."

He proceeded to take out one of those accordion type file things.

"Oh shit, fuck, damn, piss…" Fowler said and stuffed the file back into his briefcase.

"What's the matter?" I said.

"I'm sorry. I brought the wrong fuckin' file. Shit," he said and slammed his briefcase shut. "I'll have to come back."

"No sweat. I don't care." I gave him a half smile. "I got donuts. Want one?"

"Why the fuck not?" He exhaled. I had a box with the three types of donuts. Powdered, cinnamon and plain. Fowler took a powdered. Half of the powder seemed to fall off on to his grey suit.

"Oh fuck. I'm supposed to be in court this afternoon." He rubbed at the powder, which only spread the stain across his suit jacket. "Shit, fuck me!"

He took a bite, and the powder formed a circle around his lips like a clown in mid makeup. He opened the briefcase again and was fumbling through his files some more.

"Shit, I forgot it," he repeated.

One of the files had the Western Massachusetts logo on it.

"You know any lawyers who went to Western Mass?" I asked, trying to make conversation.

"You mean beside me?" It came out somewhat garbled as he was mid bite. The white circle around his lips widened. He took another bite and more powder fell on his jacket. "Fuck," he said.

I sipped my coffee.

"You went there? No shit?" I said. "You weren't classmates with the Florida governor, were you?" I said.

"Sure was." He helped himself to another powdered donut. More landed on his jacket, and he managed to spray some on his tie. He wiped at it, and, true to form, made it worse. "Fuck," he said.

"Really? Did you know him?"

"It was a small law school. Everyone knew everyone," he said through donut number two. "He was a cokehead. Left after a year. He was a creep back then. Sure wasn't the hard-right conservative back then."

This was getting interesting.

"What else about him do you remember."

"Not much. He got into drugs. Flunked just about everything, and then his daddy came and got him. He went into the service and then went to Florida State. I think they wanted to make the drug stuff go away."

"Yeah, makes sense. Did you like Western?"

"It was okay. Pittsfield isn't exactly a cultural hub. It's a fuckin arm pit."

"I know."

We chatted a bit more. Fowler finished his second donut and his coffee and looked down at his jacket and tie and shook his head.

"Fuck me," he said and headed out.

38

W ikipedia confirmed the governor went to Western Massachusetts for a year, then entered the service during the Iraq conflict, was discharged, and enrolled in Florida State University where he met his wife, Laura.

It didn't mention flunking out or him being addicted. It mentioned he was a right-wing conservative, opposed to abortion, strong second amendment advocate, an evangelical Christian, and liked to hunt. They mentioned he was in his third term and was exploring a presidential run. It said he enjoyed Florida State football, was a fitness nut who did CrossFit, and had completed three Ironman competitions.

In other words, it didn't tell me he was doing anything other than living the right-wing American dream. This was Wikipedia after all, and not exactly the dark web.

Maybe Ky didn't see what he thought he saw. Ky wasn't exactly Mister Face the Nation. And maybe the mind associates with the recent and the familiar, so Ky's mind tricked him. Maybe the sweatshirt with the emblem was close to the college emblem, and again, Ky associated the two.

Still, I had no reason to believe Ky was wrong either. Ky was sharp. He was energetic, maybe more like frenetic, but he wasn't dumb. Maybe I went with what he believed because I wanted desperately to have something.

What did I actually know?

Ali went to a sober house and Florida and split.

There was a mass shooting and a bombing, and because Ali was angry and split, she was a person of interest.

Bopp visited sober houses.

Bopp brought something to a guy in a motel who appeared to be in a tryst with a young woman, and that man was picked up in a Serenity Acres van.

Ali was on the run and scared.

Her mom was shot and Ali was back on the run.

What connected all of this?

Drugs, addiction, sex, probably money and illegal ways to get it. Power? The power to exploit weak and vulnerable people and accomplish all of these at once? The thrill of breaking the rules, getting what you want, actually taking what you want because you can.

Is that what drove people?

I believe it is what draws evil people.

A right-wing governor would fit my image of that. But was that fair? Sure, he stood for things I found distasteful, but did that make him capable of the heinous things I assigned to him? Could he be a guy who struggled in his early twenties, turned it around and dedicated himself to public service and felt driven to go as far as he could? That's George W. Bush, isn't it? That's Mitt Romney, isn't it? That's Bill Clinton?

I found politics distasteful, but that doesn't mean politicians are without morals. No one is one thing.

My phone rang.

"Duff, this is TJ."

I gulped a little.

"Yeah?"

"Got the forensic accounting report. I'm not supposed to share this, but it is public information, at least to a degree. The Florida shell company is owned by a second shell company in the Caymans."

"We knew that, didn't we?" I said.

"The principle investors of the Cayman shell company are the governor's wife and a man named Donald Bopp. In effect, the governor owns the rehabs."

"So, why the secrecy? I mean, why would you hide owning something that is supposed to do people good?"

"Because they are under investigation for Medicaid fraud, drug distribution, human trafficking and fostering prostitution."

"All having to do with the Serenity Acres?"

"Yeah, but the center of the investigation was the two houses that were destroyed and where all the evidence and witnesses were." TJ paused for breath. "The terrorist acts set the investigation back six months. Key witnesses ready to turn evidence are dead. Files are burnt and people have disappeared."

"How convenient," I said.

39

____

The two o'clock group filed in and were all in place by 2:26. All had their coffee in place, and they had exchanged greetings. Ky updated everyone on Ali.

"I can't tell if the girl is all delusional because of the shit or if she's really in trouble with those men from the treatment place," he said.

"What's that mean?" Kay asked.

"She's on the run and fearin' for her life, but the girl is high all the time, so I can't say for sure what is true and what is drug crazy shit," Ky said.

"I remember I got paranoid as hell, but some of my fears were true. Just because you're addicted doesn't mean everything you think of is wrong," Carl said.

"Word," Ky said.

"What do you all know about Ali's mom?" I asked. Ky and I made contact, and for a moment I thought he was afraid I was going to say too much about last night.

"She's an addict. I know that much," Kay said.

"What did Ali say about her? Like, did she work?" I said.

"She worked a register at a grocery store. She worked at the nursing home. She mostly got DSS," Ky said.

"Welfare," I said. "So, they would know about her."

"Shit, DSS gets your whole history. I remember that assessment. Damn, they had to know everything about you. Jobs, bank accounts, arrests, drug history." Kay rolled her eyes.

"Like addicts ever have anything left in a bank account." Carl laughed.

"So, if she was on welfare and addicted, she would've had to be in treatment somewhere," I said.

"Just like all of us. At least in the beginning," Juan said.

"Yeah, yeah, that's right." A light bulb went off in my head. "So DSS and the whatever clinic she went to would know about her."

"She probably had a record, too. I don't know no addict from the 'hood who never got arrested for somethin,'" Ky said.

The group finished up talking about heading to a NA meeting that night and where they'd be headed. Ky stuck around, and I poured him more coffee.

"Damn, D. I thought you were getting ready to talk about what we saw. Damn, you had me scared," he said.

"There's got to be something about Pittsfield, right?"

"Got to," Ky said.

"We got to find out more about Elaina. We got the cops, the welfare department or the clinics."

"How we gonna get that info. It's all protected, right?"

"Supposed to be. There's always a way."

"Your cop friend, Detective Kelley, gonna help?"

I laughed.

"He's barely speaking to me. I can't ask him now."

We were quiet for a bit.

"You got any counselin' connections over there?"

"I don't think so."

"Pittsfield DSS?"

"No, definitely not."

We sat there without saying a word. I didn't have any ideas.

"D, you hooked up with Trina again, right?"

That stopped me cold.

"How'd you know about that?" I asked.

"Never mind how. Words get around."

"So, why are you asking?" I said, realizing there was a little annoyance in my tone.

"She still official with the clinic, right? She'd have access to Ali's records."

"You're saying, ask her to make a call and ask?"

Ky shrugged.

"That could cost her job. That's illegal."

Ky shrugged.

"Would she do it for you?" Ky looked at me.

I didn't know what to say.

40

───────

It didn't feel right, and I wasn't sure why. I played fast and loose with official regulations when I worked at the clinic all the time. The difference was it was me. Trina took confidentiality seriously. This was asking someone else to do something against their values.

It didn't feel right.

It also didn't feel right because Trina and I just renewed our…our…thing of ours. Man, it sounded like a mafia thing.

Still, Ali was in trouble and in danger. The rationalization wheels were in motion. Their engine in my mind was pretty powerful, and I knew what I was going to do. There was no reason to put it off because I knew I was eventually going to do it.

"Jewish Unified Services." Trina's upbeat salutation hadn't changed.

It dawned on me this was the first time I had physically called the place since I quit. It gave me a weird feeling.

"I got a favor to ask, and you don't have to do it," I said.

"How may I help?" Trina said. It sounded like she wasn't

alone and didn't want whoever was around to know she was talking to me. She didn't let on it was me who was on the phone. I was beyond a persona non grata at the clinic.

"Can you get Ali's DSS record for me?" I asked.

There was a long pause. It was way longer than it should be.

"Ok, thank you very much," Trina said.

She hung up.

She couldn't talk. Claudia the boss might have been in earshot, or even the other counselor, Monique. Turning over records was a violation of privacy, and it was actually a crime. I may have not cared about that, but Trina needed that job, and she never was as cynical as I was.

I cruised through the afternoon, doing the mindless bartending things I did day in and day out. I tried to not think at all and let the bottle cleaning, sweeping, mopping and kitchen activities lull me into a trance. Elvis provided the soundtrack, and it was the music from 1969. As "Only the Strong Survive" transitioned to "From a Jack to King" to "Long Black Limousine" the early afternoon gave way to the late afternoon and then the early evening.

Jerry Number Two came in. I gave him his Cosmo and let him read his Bukowski book. TC was next and got his Coors' Light and B&B. Then Rocco. Rocco meant the lack of conversation was about to end. He got his Dewar's.

"Well, it was bound to happen." He often started a night with a line like this. No one ever failed to engage it.

"What's that Roc?" TC got it over with.

"Canada is at it again." For reasons known only to himself, Rocco didn't trust our neighbors to the north.

"How's that?" TC said without enthusiasm.

"Changing the football team names. Eskimos are now Elk." Rocco put his rocks glass down with extra emphasis.

"Why does this have your shorts in a twist?" Jerry Number Two had taken over response duties from TC.

"What was wrong with Eskimos? Canada has 'em." Rocco responded.

"I think it is part of the movement to not name sports team after indigenous people," Jerry Number Two.

"Maybe the Eskimos liked the honor," Rocco said in defense. "Florida State got permission from the Seminole Tribe to use their guy on the horse."

"Maybe they couldn't get the Eskimos to agree," TC said. He slid his empty B & B to me.

"Primadonnas…"

"The Eskimos or the Canadians?" Jerry Number Two said.

"Never mind…" Rocco ended the argument. He appeared quite unsatisfied.

Thankfully, Kyrone came in. His usual frenetic pace was upped a notch. He came to the end of the bar. I knew he had something to say.

"She's going back to Florida," he said. I didn't have to ask who. "Going to another Serenity Acres."

"For treatment?" I asked.

"I doubt it. She going back so they don't kill her."

41

______

Kelley was in a bit later that night. I didn't want to annoy him. Shit, I never wanted to annoy him, but he was my main source of criminal information. I gave him his Bud Light.

"What's up?" I said by way of greeting.

"Well, I hate to support your crime stopper hobby, but the thing you may or may not have seen in Pittsfield remains unsolved. We got a bulletin on today. They're asking for BOLO stuff," he said.

"BOLO? Isn't that when you can get a second pair of cheap sneakers for the same price?"

"Funny, asshole. Be On the Look Out." Kelley sounded it out.

"Ahh…does that mean you're part of it?"

"Not really, except to keep my eyes open." Kelley finished his beer, and I got him another. Rocco needed a refill; the Jerry's were all set and TC had already split.

The door open and in walked Bopp. No suit this time, instead he wore a leather car coat with black jeans. His sleek black leather gloves matched the coat.

It was unusual for him to come in at night. I got a coffee cup for him. Al came out of his cubby and immediately started to bark and snarl.

"What the fuck's his problem?" Bopp said before even saying hello.

"Al! Enough!" I yelled. Al cooled his jets and started a low growl. "What brings you in so late?"

"I wanted to let you know you girl is back with us." he said without a smile.

Al barked again.

"Can you shut that fuckin' mutt up?" he said.

I didn't care for the term "mutt."

"He's not a mutt. He's a purebred." I said with a bit of attitude. Al barked again.

"Look, this time you don't need to be making any Florida trips to check on your girl. She's in good hands." Bopp said. He smiled out of the corner of his mouth.

Something cold ran through me. I wondered how he knew we went to Florida.

"Don't bother denying anything. It wouldn't be in your best interest to go to Florida. Got me?" Bopp said and gave me a nod to say did I understand.

Al barked again, and I yelled again. He picked up the pace and continued to yell.

"Hey, Donnie, let me tell you something. If I want to go to Florida, I'll go to fucking Florida or, for that matter, anywhere else," I said. The bar conversations stopped, and I could feel eyes on me.

Al was barking out of his mind now.

Bopp looked at me hard, and when he went to put his hand on his hip, I could see a holster. It might have been intentional.

Al kept at it. Agnes came out and started to howl at the same time.

"You might want to think that over, Duffy." He leaned in a bit.

Somebody turned off the TV.

I got that feeling I get when it is almost time. I was trying to keep it under wraps. Al kept barking.

"First, I'm gonna kick this fuckin' dog to shut up!" He turned toward Al.

That was it.

Bopp reared back to drive a boot at Al.

I went over the top of the bar and body blocked Bopp. He went hard into the wall.

Something went bad inside me. Years ago, a biker broke some of Al's ribs with a kick. The memory lived inside of me, not as a memory but almost as a physical thing.

I drove two body shots into Bopp and heard a sick noise come out of him. I flurried a series of upper cuts into his body and could feel the rage surge in me. I came up with a right hook and followed it with a straight left that exploded his nose.

I grabbed him by his leather collar and put my face into his.

"You know what happened to the last guy who kicked Al? I beat him to fucking death!" I slammed his head into the wall.

He reached for the gun, but I was slamming him repeatedly into the wall, and it spilled across the floor.

The sight of the gun set me off, and I rained punches on him. He began to go limp. Then I got hit from behind.

"Jesus Christ, Duffy, you're going to kill him!" It was Kelley, and he was on top of me. Rocco was next to him and had the gun in his hand. They were both there the night I killed the biker.

"Calm the fuck down!" Kelley yelled.

Bopp wiped at his bloody face and headed toward the door, righting himself with help from the wall as he walked.

My chest was heaving.

Al had stopped barking for the moment and walked over and sniffed at me. He whined a bit, and I touched his head lightly.

The memory of the time I beat the biker came back. It was more than a memory; it was physical. I had to concentrate to not vomit.

42

"God damn, Duff, you're lucky I don't arrest you," Kelley said. It brought me out of my trance.

"He was going to kick Al. He had a gun. He threatened me. What else do I need to know?" I said. My shirt was soaked with sweat, and I wiped my forehead with my sleeve. I had chills running through me, and I felt cold and hot at the same time.

"And if I didn't tackle you? You would have beat him to death," Kelley glared at me for a long moment. "That's murder."

My mind drifted back to the biker. He had hurt Al real bad. I blacked out while I was hitting him, and I can still see the blood spurting out of him with each strike. I still had nightmares about taking a life with my bare hands.

The guy deserved it, but it wasn't my justice to hand out, or maybe it was, but the sentence I imposed was way too harsh. It was something I didn't like living with.

"Hey, Kelley, you want this?" Rocco motioned the gun to Kelley, handle first.

Kelley took it delicately with two fingers. I guessed because he didn't want to leave prints even though Rocco had had his hands all over it.

I set everyone up with a drink and poured myself four fingers of Jim Beam.

"Why did that guy just leave?" Jerry Number Two said.

"Probably the gun, the threat, and, who knows what else, that he didn't want coming out if he'd gotten taken down to the station for a statement," Kelley said.

Al and Agnes walked out to the bar and looked at me.

Al gave me one bark. It was different than the frenetic noise he was making before at Bopp.

"I think Al just said thanks," Jerry Number Two said.

Al turned and went to his bed. Agnes followed.

The boys finished their drinks. The adrenaline had died down. My blood pressure was almost back to normal.

Almost.

I closed up and decided to pour myself another four fingers and walk the dogs to see if I could settle my nerves. I kept to the back streets, walking down West to Bradford and over to Lincoln.

I thought about Ali.

Why the hell would she go back to Serenity Acres? Then Bopp switches personas and tries to scare me off after he let me know he knew I was in Florida.

How did he know that?

My phone pinged. It was Ky.

"You up?" it read.

I let him know I was walking the dogs.

"When are we going to Florida?" was the next text. I should have known Ky wouldn't let this go.

Al was sniffing a bush on the corner of Lincoln and South Allen. Agnes sniffing the base of a stop sign.

"D?" was the next text. Ky wasn't patient, and he certainly was persistent.

"I don't know if that's such a good idea." I texted him back. "Maybe she's back in treatment getting sober."

Ky didn't respond.

I felt lousy bowing out on him. After Kelley's latest lecture, it was maybe sinking in I needed to stop my Robin Hood ways. Maybe someday, I would kill someone, go to jail, and really screw up my life. Maybe, because of me, someone would really get hurt or in trouble.

Maybe.

"You are giving up," was the next text. There was no question mark. It was a statement from Ky.

I headed back to the apartment. The dogs were slow, but they headed in the right direction now.

Giving up.

Giving up?

A long time ago, someone asked me why I threw myself into situations like this. I told them I didn't like it when vulnerable people were being taken advantage. I said I liked helping the people no one else was going to help.

I texted Ky.

"We'll fly out in the morning," was what I wrote.

43

We landed and rented a car like the last time we came to Florida. Ky kept his headphones on the whole flight, and he seemed even more nervous than the last time. He kept them on until we got in the Chevy Impala.

"You okay? I asked.

"Am now. Don't think flying is something I'll ever get used to," Ky said.

"What's the plan?" I asked.

"I thought you had a plan. You're the chief of this shit."

"Chief, huh?" I gave that some thought. "I say we cruise by the sober houses and see if there's anything to see."

"Sounds good," Ky said.

I didn't think it sounded so good. If the goal was to find Ali, I doubted she'd be hanging outside one of the houses gardening or shooting hoop in the backyard. She'd be inside, and I bet they —whoever they were—would be keeping close tabs on her.

There were three sober houses in Sarasota and two in Venice. We drove by the first one in Sarasota and parked across the street. It was in a lower middle-class neighborhood and looked like a prefab double wide. The subtle SE in script was just above the numbers on the left side of the front door.

Ky and I sat in silence for fifteen minutes. It wasn't like Ky to be quiet for that long. At the half an hour mark, no one had come in or out. There was no noise coming from the house and no activity in the surrounding houses and, except for a handful of cars going back and forth to go to work or grocery shopping, nothing was out of place.

"Maybe we should go check out another house," I said.

"Word," Ky said.

The second place in Sarasota was the same type of house with the same SE initials to left of the front door and with the exact same amount of activity going, which was to say there was no activity. We gave this one twenty minutes.

"Let's go on to Venice," I said.

"Yeah, I'm starting to feel a little stupid doing this," Ky said.

Venice was the same story. Same type houses, same type initials, no activity. We left watching the first house after a half an hour and went on to the second with the same results.

Nothing.

It was now early afternoon. The sun was obnoxiously bright, and I was tired. My back was cramping from sitting and doing nothing. We were sitting outside the last house in Venice.

"So, if Ali be down here, how we going to get to her? Park outside of these five houses and wait for her to emerge? This shit is whack," Ky said.

"You got a better idea?"

"You da chief."

"I didn't feel like no chief last night when you were saying we had to come down here. Who knows where she is, who even knows what we're up against?" I had more annoyance in my tone than I wanted.

"You know, D—Hold up." Ky motioned with his chin. "It's the fat brother with the sailor cap."

A white mini-van with the Serenity Acres logo had pulled up. It was the black guy with the sailor cap, and he tooted the horn twice. In about a minute, a young, frail, light-skinned black woman trotted to the minivan. She had on a simple black hoodie, matching black sweatpants, and white Crocs.

"There she go," Ky said. "What do we do now?"

"We follow," I said.

I did my best to tail my sailor friend without being noticed. We tried to stay two cars back, but I hit a red light and wound up four or five cars back. I started to panic a bit.

"Damn, D, we gonna lose them!" Ky said. I wasn't the only one who panicked.

We came to a four-way stop, and I had no idea which way they went.

"Take a right," Ky said. "This is starting to look familiar."

I went with Ky's instincts. I didn't have any better plan.

"Yup, D! Just what I thought!"

"What? I don't get it." I said.

Ky pointed ahead and slightly to the left.

"There it go, right there D!"

Up ahead, three hundred feet to the left was the Ocean View Motor Inn.

44

———

I pulled up across the street. As I did, the minivan pulled out and headed back in the direction in which we came. Just the driver this time, no Ali in the van.

"They turned her out. They fuckin' turnin' Ali out," Ky said. "We gotta stop this shit.

"Calm down, let's think this through. We don't want to run in there half crazy. Let's—" My phone pinged with a text. It was from Trina. "Hold on."

The text read:

"This might be what you were looking for. I hope it's worth it because if I get caught, I'll lose my job."

Below the text was a photo taken from a cell phone of a computer screen. It took me a second to realize what it was.

"Holy shit! Holy fuckin' shit. He's going to kill her!"

I jumped out of the car and ran to the last room on the left wing of the building. Ky caught up to me at the door. I didn't break stride and jumped, kicking the door in with a flying sidekick. It flew open and broke off at the lower hinge.

I heard a scream. It was Ali.

She was in the corner of the room, crying and shaking hysterically.

In front of her was the governor, holding a gun and now pointing it at me.

We startled him, but he regained his exposure.

"You again. You don't get it. You can't leave shit alone." He gritted his teeth and steadied the gun at us.

"I know." I stared back at him. The same feeling that ran through my veins last night was back. The difference this time was I had a gun pointed at me from eight feet away.

"It's over governor. I know your story," I said.

Ky had a bewildered look on his face.

"You don't know shit." He tried to smile it off.

"I know you own the shell companies that run this bullshit treatment program. I know you're exploiting the insurance benefits of the girls. I know you're keeping them high, selling shit, and turning them out."

"You're full of shit. You don't know shit," he said. He tried to look relaxed, but it didn't work.

"I know you spent a year at Western Massachusetts Law where you ran with the inner-city drug crowd. That is until your daddy got you out and out of the trouble," I said.

"Shut up! Shut up! Just shut up!" He lifted the gun and aimed.

"And I know you got Elaina Estime pregnant." A look came over his face. I thought he was going to be sick. With Ali in the room, I wasn't sure I could say it.

"I know Ali is your daughter. That's why you killed Elaina and why you were going to kill Ali. You'd never get elected if everyone really knew you. It is all going to come out."

He aimed.

"Get ready to die…" He pointed at me. He aimed.

Ali let out a scream like I never heard before and threw her body into him. It jarred him, but he held the gun. I stepped in and threw a hook that dropped the scumbag hard. The gun banged to the floor.

Ky dove at it but couldn't grab it. Instead, he hit it forward. The governor grabbed it, righted himself and shook off the cobwebs.

"You assholes, you're all going to die." He extended the gun and grimaced as he pulled the trigger.

I closed my eyes and heard a burst of gunfire. I dove to the ground and landed on Ky, who had dove before me. Ali was screaming. All we could hear were Ali's screams.

The burst lasted no longer than ten seconds. Neither Ky nor I moved for much longer than that.

"You hit?" Ky said.

"No, you?" I said. I rolled off Ky and jumped to my feet. The governor was on his back on the bed, bleeding from gunshot wounds to his chest. His chest didn't move.

"On the ground! On the ground! All three of you! Hands out in front of you! Don't move!"

Three figures holding automatic weapons were in the room, weapons raised as they surveyed the room in different directions.

"Clear!" one of them shouted, and they relaxed the weapons. The one who shouted approached the governor. He shook his head at the others. "Dead."

One of the figures removed the helmet and googles on his head.

Except it wasn't a he. It was a woman.

It was TJ.

45

I ran to Ali ,and she wrapped her arms around me so hard she almost suffocated me.

"Duffy...Duffy..." She kept crying. She was hyperventilating and shaking. I looked over at Kyrone and motioned him over with my head. He took over the hugging duties. I stepped back and made eye contact with TJ.

"You okay?" She said.

I couldn't speak for a long moment. I cough my breath.

"What the hell is going on? Why are you here?"

"Detective Kelley called this morning. The gun you took off Bopp was the gun that killed Elaina Estime. Kelley knew you had headed back down here and checked the flight manifests. He knew you were in danger and called us. We followed you since you got the rental car.

"I never saw you," I said.

"We do this shit for a living, unlike some other people." TJ half smiled.

I didn't say anything for a long moment. I surveyed the room and had that familiar feeling of it being too real and not real at all.

I looked back hat TJ.

"Um, thanks," I said. "You know, for saving my life…again."

TJ smiled.

"You got any idea why he was gonna kill this woman?"

I thought it over and realized I was going to be telling this story a lot for a few days.

"Yeah, I do." I took a breath and tried to be as succinct as possible. "The governor and his partner owned Serenity Acres. They were running A Florida Shuffle"

"Yeah, we were involved because there were suspicions of human trafficking."

"That's right," I said. "Looks like they got greedy. In addition to exploiting the girl's benefits, keeping them addicted, then turning them out, the stiff over there liked to have sex with them."

"Doesn't line up real well with a presidential campaign, does it?"

"That was the problem. Ali didn't want any part of what was going, and split as soon as she could. Somebody must've looked at the fact she was born in Pittsfield. That's why Elaina Estime was killed."

"And the mass shooting?"

"I'm guessing that was a setup so they could kill Ali without anyone wondering why."

"How did you find out Ali was the daughter?"

I didn't say anything.

"Um, lucky guess?" I said and smiled.

"Yeah, we'll leave that alone for now." She exhaled in frustration. "Why did she come back to Florida?"

"Not sure, but ask Bopp. They might've got her hooked again and made promises," I said.

"Did she know she was his daughter?"

"No, she thought she was coming to have sex with him. That was part of the deal."

"Except he was going to shoot her," TJ said and nodded.

"Yeah, it is some fucked up shit."

I turned and looked at Ky. He was holding Ali. Her crying had slowed, but she still held on tight.

TJ looked over at the dead body and shook her head.

"This is going to be a shit show soon. The media, the locals, the Feds..."

"Can you guys control any of that?" I asked.

She looked at me and didn't answer. She waited and looked at her partners who had drifted outside the door.

"Sometimes, if something could affect national security, it, uh, may get less attention than one might think." She gave me that look which said to not ask anything else. "You'll be going back to Crawford, right? In case we need to find you?"

I nodded.

"How's Agnes?" For the first time switching to the personal.

"She's great. She loves hanging with Al in the bar."

"Thank you for taking care of her." She looked down for a second. "Um, I don't know if I ever said this but, when it comes to me and you and how I...I'm sorry."

She turned and walked out.

46

Two men in dark suits and sunglasses came in shortly after that. They were both about six feet tall and a hundred eighty pounds. They were both white, one with angular features and dark hair parted on the left. The other had softer features, light brown hair and a receding hairline.

They motioned for TJ and her two partners to leave the room. Two more men in laundry uniforms came in, took the governor's body and the bloody sheets and put them in oversized laundry bags together. They headed out of the room, leaving Ali, Ky, and me.

Dark hair spoke.

"There will be a media release about the governor later today. It will say he committed suicide. In the coming months, Serenity Acres will be quietly shuttered. We are prepared to offer you flights home and, if need be, cover stories for what happened in the last forty-eight hours, though we don't think that will be necessary. I don't mean to be cryptic, but in the interest of national security, there isn't anything more I can say."

Light hair took a turn.

"Donald Bopp is in federal custody for the murder of Elaina Estime. You will probably not hear any news coverage about that."

Dark hair took back over.

"The three of you could be turned over to Florida officials and be charged with several crimes. You don't want that. We don't want that. It is imperative you tell no one of what happened here."

"Clear?" Light hair said and made contact with each of us separately and deliberately.

"Your rental is on its way back to the airport. We will see you get the next flight back home to Crawford," Dark hair said.

The three of us didn't speak. We just nodded.

We were about to head out of the room when Dark Hair put his hand on my forearm. He looked at Ky and me.

"It isn't lost on us your work, uh, as unconventional as it was, did Homeland Security a great favor. It hastened the end of some evil shit we had been trying to close down." He sort of half smiled.

"It took a lot of balls too."

PART III

47

———————

It had been three weeks since Florida. Ali came to the two o'clock group every day and said she hadn't used yet. Ky brought her to the meetings and took her home, and they were going to Twelve-Step meetings at night. My fingers were crossed.

It was just after the two o'clock meeting broke up with just Rocco and me in the bar, and Trina walked in. It was the first time I'd seen her since I asked her to do me the favor.

"We okay?" I asked.

"Yeah, we're okay." Trina said, but didn't smile. Rocco was halfway down the bar and Fox news was covering Trina and my conversation.

"Um, Ali's okay?" She said.

"So far, seems to be. She was here today and is starting to look better," I said.

"Ends justifying the means…" she said. "Can I have a wine?"

I poured her a Pinot Grigio.

"I know what I asked you was a lot and—-" she stopped me.

"It's fine, but let's stop talking about it."

I nodded.

"I know Kelley called TJ, and I know she did something to save you again." She struggled a bit with her words.

"I'm not supposed to talk about what happened. I—" Trina interrupted.

"I don't care about what happened," she sipped her wine. "I want to know something, and you need to tell me. You need to be honest. You owe me that." Trina put her wine down and looked me hard in the eye.

I nodded.

"Will it always be her?" She kept the look right at me. That's all she said, but I understood.

"No, not anymore. Not since, well, I guess three weeks ago when you stopped in," I said.

She allowed herself a half smile.

"Good," she said and finished her wine.

She winked at me and headed out.

DUFFY'S FIGHT CLUB

Join "Duffy's Fight Club" for free short thrillers, an audio book, Tom's magazine work, a video on judging boxing, Tom's appearance on "Copy Cat Killers" and Rocky the blood hound singing "My Way."
TomSchreck.com.

ABOUT THE AUTHOR

TOM SCHRECK is the author of Amazon's number-one hard-boiled mystery, *The Vegas Knockout*. He counts Robert B. Parker, John D. MacDonald, J.A. Konrath, Reed Farrel Coleman, Ken Bruen and Michael Connelly among his favorite crime fiction authors and his Duffy Dombrowski series has been referred to as "As good or better as the early Spenser." He is a columnist with *Westchester Magazine* and a frequent contributor to *Crimespree Magazine*, *Referee*, and other publications.

Follow Tom and Subscribe to updates at
TomSchreck.com

BOOKS BY TOM SCHRECK

www.ingramcontent.com/pod-product-compliance
Lightning Source LLC
Chambersburg PA
CBHW021127070726
47591CB00014B/1685